"Roy Parvin writes like an angel. His stories are deep and dark, rich with metaphor, shot through with grizzly humor, playful, intense, strange. His prose is rhythmic and dense, intoxicating but never inaccessible. There's little to say except that he hears the music, always in his head. And he loves words, loves the way they jangle together, loves the obscure detail, the minorly tragic, the moment when the small ugly thing turns, for only an instant, strong and beautiful, loves the edges and courts them, relentlessly in every line.

"He is driven by the cadence he hears in his head, he is a slave to that music, he loves words, loves story, like other men love cars and women, and the result of that passion is stories that are always fresh, always surprising, deeply satisfying, and almost too beautiful to bear.

"His work makes me sorry I'm not a publisher, makes me glad to be a writer, even gladder to be a reader, makes me remember all the things about words and storytelling that I truly love."

—PAM HOUSTON

The Loneliest Road
in America

The Loneliest Road
in America

STORIES BY ROY PARVIN

CHRONICLE BOOKS
SAN FRANCISCO

Some of these stories originally appeared in slightly different
form in the following publications: "The Loneliest Road in America"
in *Alaska Quarterly Review*; "Darkness Runs" in *Northwest Review*;
"Smoke" in *High Plains Literary Review*; "A Dream She Had" in *Fourteen
Hills*; "Ice the Color of Sky" in *Nimrod* (and winner of the *Nimrod*:
Katherine Anne Porter Prize in Fiction); "May" in *The Writing Path 2:
An Anthology of New Writing from Writers' Conferences and Festivals*
(University of Iowa Press); "Between Knowing and Dying" in
The Quarterly; "It's Me Again" in *Turnstile*; "Fish Story" in *South
Dakota Review*; "The Ames Coil" in *Epoch*.

Library of Congress Cataloging-in-Publication Data:

Parvin, Roy.
        The loneliest road in America: stories / by Roy Parvin
                p.   cm.
        Contents: The loneliest road in America—Darkness runs—Smoke—
        A dream she had—Ice the color of sky—Trapline—May—Between
        knowing and dying—It's me again—Fish story—The Ames coil.
        ISBN 0-8118-1435-1
        1. Trinity Alps Region (Calif.)—Social life and customs—Fiction.
        2. California, Northern—Social life and customs—Fiction.
        3. City and town life—California, Northern—Fiction.   I. Title.
PS3566.A7726L66   1997
813'.54—dc20   96-41761
                                          CIP

Book and cover design: Gretchen Scoble
Cover photograph: Jonathan Safir/photonica

Printed in the United States of America

Distributed in Canada by Raincoast Books
8680 Cambie Street
Vancouver, B.C. V6P 6M9

10 9 8 7 6 5 4 3 2 1

Chronicle Books
85 Second Street
San Francisco, CA 94105

Web Site: www.chronbooks.com

I am indebted to the following texts for the help they provided in writing "Darkness Runs" and "Fish Story": *Wintu Texts* (Alice Shephard), *Wintu Dictionary* (Harvey Pitkin), *The Way We Lived* (Malcolm Margolin), and *Handbook of the Indians of California* (A. L. Kroeber).

Thanks to Peter Schwartz, Danny Mitchell, Erik Migdail, and Susan Ristow for reading early versions of these stories. I'm grateful for the unflagging support of Leigh Feldman, my agent, and lucky to have such a wise, generous editor in Jay Schaefer. Finally, I cannot imagine a better teacher or friend than Pam Houston, a boundless source of inspiration in life and on the page.

To Janet

And in memory of my father,
the biggest man I'll ever know

Contents

The Loneliest Road in America

IT WAS THE YEAR I grew as big as the trees. When Galen saw me stretching at the sky like that, my arms and legs gone stringy as some kind of crazy bean, when he saw that, he thought it was high time he taught me his pitches. I was sixteen years old.

It was just the two of us in those secret woods, Galen and me. I'd run miles past Goldfield campground, all the way to where the road ended, as far as it went. And when I'd finally stopped running, I saw this was where I was, the middle of nowhere, a swale deep inside wilderness and forest service lands, an old patented gold mine gone to rust, a place not on any map. Galen had showed me the old tailing carts buried in the ground; it reminded me of dinosaur bones I'd seen in a schoolbook.

"Kit," he said to me. It was May and the dogwood blooms were big as headlights. I had to lean in to hear him. All the rains that year—the melt was bigger than usual. Boulder Creek spilled out like a faucet jammed all the way on. "Kit," he said, "you got the arm of a young Sandy Koufax." He put the squeeze above my elbow. "Boy, if I'm lying, I'm dying," he said. "Sandy Koufax."

I hadn't had much truck with baseball before then. It seemed only a game to me and I never had time for games since I slugged Paulie Aven in the seventh grade for making fun of my dead ma and they put me away on account of that and some other troubles I'd had. I remembered throwing the ball a few times before then with my daddy, but I was only a kid and all I could remember of it was trying to throw it way up high, he was that tall. We did play some baseball at juvie center. But the idea there was to aim at the batter's head and the games ended quickly, an inning at the most.

"Show me your stuff," Galen said to me. I tossed a number of fist-sized river rocks for him. "A girl," he said. "That's what you throw like. A girl." He pulled at his beard, which was greasy and black and silvery in parts. "I can fix that," he said.

He had me throw one hundred rocks a day. After May was done I was able to whistle rocks clear down the hill, across Boulder Creek. From up there on the crest the water looked pop-bottle green.

When Galen saw me winging the rocks that far, all the way across the river, he knew it was time. "I had command of five pitches," he said. He walked around the ponderosa. The nubbin that was his left arm, his pitching arm, what remained of it, hitched up in jerks.

He hadn't talked a lot about his days before the accident. What I knew was that it was lightning that had knocked him out of that Douglas fir he was limbing, a rogue shock that lopped off his arm, knocked him out of the life he thought was his. I understood how a person might not want to talk about something that couldn't be taken back, how there was no use in it, only sadness.

Galen was up the trunk of that fir when the gullywasher spun down off Billy's Peak, a purple-black top. He flew right out of his spurs, sailed thirty yards. The spurs still gripped the trunk, way up there, like an old promise. "Messed up my internal thermostat but good," was practically all he'd say about it. That explained why he walked those woods jaybird naked, only a coonskin tail on him, not his head, but around his waist, trailing down over his heinie. "Haven't been cold since 1961," he'd say, then get a wet look in his eyes and seem real far away even though he was right there.

He paced off sixty feet from the ponderosa now, had me throw at the trunk. "Five pitches," he said. "That's what I had, boy. A speedball. Uncle Charley, my curve. An off-speed to keep them honest. A sinker that liked to fall off the table, it dropped so much."

"That's four," I said. "I thought you said five. Thought you said you had five pitches."

"I did," he said. And that was all he said on that. I didn't press further. These were his woods, had been since the lightning, twenty-five years before. I was thankful enough for him letting me hole up there.

At first, back when I'd run from what I did to Foster Bob on the trail, late March, I was sure I was alone, nothing but me and all those trees. Then one day in April I was trapping brown trout between the rocks in Boulder Creek, splashing in the shallows.

"That's a sporting concept if ever I seen one," he'd said. I near jumped out of the creek, the jolt of him standing there naked, his beard wild as manzanita, only eyes and nose visible. "You could seine for them browns," he said. "Won't get chilled to the bone that way, neither."

We'd studied the other. I considered he knew about what I did to Foster Bob. But that didn't seem right. There was a skin of ice on the madrone trunks, it was that cold, and he hadn't a stitch on him, didn't look like any official far as I could tell. I rolled over the idea that maybe he had some of those notions in his head that Foster Bob did, and I looked for a rock big enough to mean business.

After a while, though, he turned and went back through the glade of dogwoods. I followed him to that hugger-mugger cabin he had hidden in the oaks on the other side of the swale and nipped behind the trees.

"I know you're out there, boy," he'd said without looking back. "You can hide or come out. Fine, either way."

"You better not try anything," I'd said. "I'm dangerous."

"Well, Katie bar the door," he said. "A desperado."

And that was how it started, how it came to be that I was standing there with Galen Deerborne now under the trees, the crickets making raggedy songs, the river washing down the canyon, me learning the fine points of gripping a ball crosswise, even though it was just rocks I was throwing.

I had a pile heaped that I'd carried up from Boulder Creek. One by one I hurled them at the ponderosa. "Snap it off, Kit," he said when I tried an Uncle Charley. "Lookit that movement, boy," he said after the rock flew, a bird with a broken wing. He clapped his hand, the one he had left, against the skin of his hip. "Christ on a crutch. You'll be a bonus baby yet."

The puzzle bark was rasped up, an underbelly of tree showing. I did a full windup, arms reaching overhead forming a steeple, the way he taught me, coming back down, a full-stop rest, the ball on my hip away from the batter, then arms and legs swimming to home. "Like a buggy whip," Galen said. "Now the off-speed. You want to freeze him. Get him looking like he was staring up a girlie's dress."

It went on this way, me throwing, Galen coaching, just the two of us in those woods. The day was heating up. I took off my shirt. What a sight we must have been! Galen there in the altogether. Me, spindly, a chest that was only blade and bone. It was true what he said, that if you homed in, the whole world would go away and all there'd be was that two-foot square, the strike zone. I nicked the corners, slid them right down the pipe, and I didn't think of anything else, not anything, not my daddy up in Weaverville, not them louses in juvie center, not Foster Bob, nobody.

The rock in my hand made a hearty *thwok* when it hit the meat of the tree. I made a promise to myself, what I would get, if I threw it square. I wanted something better to sleep in than the sling I'd rigged in the hanging madrone through the swale. *Thwok!* I wanted to rub away all the bad I'd done. *Thwok!* I wanted a girl or some kind of love. I wanted something that could ease what my daddy was going through. *Thwok! Thwok! Thwok!*

"That's enough," Galen said after a time and it was over too soon. "Let's soak that arm, keep it fresh." We picked our way down to the creek and I dipped my arm in the current up to my shoulder. That water wasn't too far removed from snow. It was June yet and we could still see the drifts up the canyon, between the trees, white as bedsheets. The days were getting skillet-hot but the nights could bring winter to mind quick. I'd wake up in my sling with the cold stabbing at me and think I'd need a lot more than a blanket to keep me warm.

"Tell me about the summer it snowed," I said to Galen now. The water ran around my arm and made a rip in the current.

"I already did," Galen said and gave a gray smile. "Must be fifty times now."

"I like to think about it," I said. The thought of all those pleasure boaters sliding off Slate Mountain—"ass over teakettle," Galen'd say. The thought that it was something my daddy knew, too, but didn't ever tell me, wanted to but just never got around to it. Then I thought about my daddy, him in that bed in Weaverville, the disease snapping his nerves like frayed shoelaces, and I didn't want to think about that anymore.

"Look at this," I said to Galen now. I pointed with my other arm toward the pools. There were flecks and motes of gold lolling in the shallows.

Galen said, "That there is the genuine item."

"The truth?" I said. "Gold?"

"Gospel. Years of a big melt like this one. It's nature's version of placer mining. Seen it all the time. All the way back when my pa and me used to pan here." His bum arm went flapping the way it did. "You know, Kit," he said. "I could do with a beaver cigarette now."

I rolled two the way he taught me, tearing squares off the paper bag I had in my pocket and stuffing the deal with dried leaves and duff. It made a powerful smoke.

"Just one for you, Kit. Can't break training." He winked an eye at me that was blue as heaven.

The two of us smoked the cigarettes down to the bone. Galen blew rings as the heat ran out of the day. We didn't say anything, only watched the gold in the water. It was the time of afternoon when most everything seemed good and right, and whatever didn't, well, that didn't matter just then anyway.

The gold burnished like hope. I considered all the things it could mean to a person but couldn't hardly imagine any life other than the one I owned. Even so, the dust gave a handsome glitter.

"Do you think we could . . ." I said to Galen but didn't know how to finish, there was so much I could have said, so much I wanted to cram between the start of that thought and the end of it.

"I think we could," Galen said. The river smelled fresh, cold. Everything else was colored in browns and greens, the trunks of the madrones going to peel.

What I thought of then was how far my arm could take me, all the places I knew must have existed beyond Trinity County, and I wanted to believe it was our ticket out, the both of us. I rolled another beaver smoke for Galen.

"I think we could," he said when I handed it to him, said it softer yet.

MY DADDY WAS THE tallest man in the county. Everybody knew him. They'd say, "Kit, your daddy's about bigger than a Jeffrey pine." They'd say, "That man's so big he needs a zip code of his own."

He was a big enough man to be my ma and my daddy. I never was familiar with my ma in the personal sense, and what little I did know were things I'd heard. She was half Wintun. She drank like she had a hole in her glass and had to gulp it down before it all ran out. She died when I was five, over six hundred miles away in a desert ghost town near the Nevada-California border, a place called Ryolite.

It would no doubt make a better story if I could tell a number of father and son tales. But that wasn't the way it was. The county was going to hell, the only work setting choker cable for Sierra Pacific. Those were long days of working the trees. My daddy got lazy once and the cable bit tight around some timber and snapped off the top of his pointer finger. After that he'd say, "I can count the good things about setting chokers on one hand . . ." and then he'd lift his midget finger, always a laugh in our house.

Mostly it was sunup to sundown days of work. I had my free run of the place and I grew up wild as weeds. School never did much for me, the words always looking squashed and jumbly.

I got into more scrapes than my daddy could keep track of. Even so, he never put a hand on me, not once. When I did wrong he mostly cupped his palm to the back of my head and said, "Now, Kit, you understand what you did there, son." And he always seemed somehow smaller in those times, like life was pressing him down. When that letter came from Ryolite about my ma, I watched him read it through the window and he shrunk down inside himself, didn't even look tall anymore, looked to be he was going to disappear. And I had to run all the way down to the park and swing in the jungle gym for hours, then break bottles in the gutter to get that picture out of my head.

There was one time I can remember when it seemed life might work out after all. My daddy was chip-sealing for the county roads and the pay was good and the days were short and things got pretty flush. He bought a team of coon hounds and we couldn't wait until bear season. I didn't get into any trouble that summer, just minded the six dogs, teaching them to hunt, feeding them, staking them out.

Come fall, we camped out in Eagle Creek, the dogs yippering all night long, the temperature dropping under freezing, me and my daddy in the tent. In the morning we rode out. There were dogs in the truck bed, five of them, and one staked to the hood of the old Ford. We didn't say anything driving the trail, only watched the dogs picking up the scent, the two of us smiling at the other, my daddy's long, long legs bent under the steering wheel.

It didn't last. He was out again when the rainy season came and then they shut the forest and then I slugged Paulie Aven. The last few years I didn't see my daddy much. After I got out, he was sick. Something seemed wrong even before they told him. I remember how his shoulders got so thin they couldn't balance a log on them if he'd wanted. The disease creeped down from his upper back, turning everything to dead weight.

When I found out he was going to the hospital for good, I took my bed out back, the headboard, too, and lit the mess on fire, big green and blue flames that caught the nub grass in the yard and ran clear to old man Fitzhugh's coop. It gave a sick feeling, hearing all that hen screaming, nothing I could do once the coop was lit.

After that the courts said I needed discipline in my life, that my daddy couldn't be my daddy anymore, and they gave me Foster Bob as a replacement and he was never any daddy. I lived in a closet that he said was a room and I had to work harder than any man should. "You have to be broken, son, before I can put you back together," was what he'd say. I Sheetrocked the whole third floor of his house, all the mudding, too. After I was done with that he said I didn't have to go to school anymore, said what I was learning out on his tree farm was a lot more important.

In March Foster Bob suggested we take a father-son winter camping trip up Boulder Creek trail to Goldfield. I knew it wouldn't be bear hunting with my daddy, but I looked forward to it just the same.

We snowshoed, humping packs and tents on our shoulders. It was a peaceful thing being in those woods, nobody but us. We ate lunch on a giant granite boulder.

"What do you want to be?" he'd said to me when we were done with eating.

"What do you mean?" I'd said.

"Life," he said. "You know, what you want from it."

I thought about that for a while. Nobody'd ever told me I could have a choice. I thought of what all the lowdowns in juvie center would have said, about raping girls or knocking over a store or crank, and I knew that wasn't what I wanted. Foster Bob worked on his chaw, a shaving nick on his cheek, that fat face, his thick hair blacker than shoe polish. He pulled on his gimme cap and looked me head to toe.

I said finally, "I think I want me one of those sheepherding dogs and a car, nothing fancy. I'd like to drive around the country and visit fairs and cities and go in that tunnel that I hear goes under a river. New York or somewhere. Then I'd go and see those croco-diles, see if they're as big as they say. After I do all that, I'd sit down and try to figure out what's what. What would you do?" I said.

Foster Bob got up then. I thought he was going to shake my hand. "I'm your father now," he said.

"So I hear," I said.

"How about a hug, then," he said. "The way your daddy did." Before I could even open my mouth to say my daddy never hugged me, he locked his arms around and gripped me. He said, "You're getting to be such a big boy." He ran his hands down my legs and licked my ears. He said, "I love you. I love you."

It was a weird thing. I'd heard stories in juvie center. It seemed then I wasn't in my body anymore and I'd wondered if it was going dead the way my daddy's was. Foster Bob pulled my hair back, started chewing on my neck. His voice got an edge. "Sweetness," he said. "You're going to suck my dick till my hat pops off."

It was like somebody threw a switch then. I didn't know where it came from, but my fists started raining in from everywhere. I was making gurgly noises in my throat, too. When he fell I started kick-ing and kicking and it seemed a flood was pouring out from me and every bad thing that had happened in my sorry life was in my boots and balled-up hands. I got a piece of deadfall and commenced with that, whaling on Foster Bob. By the end I was bawling like a kid and he wasn't moving any, blood coming out of his mouth and ears and nose.

And I ran. I didn't stop until I got to the swale and it seemed like it was a good place, the end of the road and into the woods. And I set up camp in the crook of a madrone and trapped squirrels and caught browns and kokanee salmon by cornering them in the rocks in Boulder Creek. I missed my daddy something awful. But the last time I saw him, in that hospital bed in Weaverville, he wasn't really my daddy anymore, was only a bag of sticks waiting to die. He tried to talk but his mouth wasn't working. I knew what he was saying anyway, what he always said whenever the money was real tight and things seemed darker than ever. "I know, Daddy," I'd said. "Throw a blanket over it, right? That's what you're saying. Throw a blanket over it." Those brown eyes of his took me in. And I knew if they could have cried, they would have.

I WAS GETTING BIGGER all the time. Galen couldn't believe it. "Boy, you're going to make the show," he said to me. "Sure as I'm standing here."

It was mid-June. I was mixing up the pitches like a bartender.

"You're painting the plate, you are," Galen said. "Never seen anything like this."

I had a wonderful feeling throwing those pitches. Galen said the rocks were making my arm stronger than anything. "Boy, you're going to set the world on fire," he said. He told me again of the plan he'd been thinking of. "They got these regional tryouts, Kit. I know you've never seen live batters, but that doesn't matter anyway. You just home in the way I taught you."

What he told me about was a whole bunch of towns I'd never heard of and parts of the country I'd only seen in books and uniforms that would be washed every day and hanging in the lockers ready for me by the time I'd get there. And the ballpark itself! There'd be pretty girls in bikini tops and organ music and hot dogs.

"It's like a carnival," I said.

"That it is," Galen said. He pointed with his good arm at the ponderosa.

I loosed a sidearm fastball and the rock exploded when it hit the trunk. It seemed the shot could have been heard all the way down past the web of trails, down at Goldfield campground, it was that loud.

"Go to the stretch, boy. Man on first and second," he said. "That's right. Look him off, look him off."

I stole a look over my shoulder, over toward where the swale dropped into a grove of sugarpines. At the stretch I looked behind me at the Douglas fir with Galen's spurs frozen in the trunk. My Uncle Charley fluttered like a butterfly.

"I swear," Galen said. "That thing could turn a corner."

Night was coming down over the Trinities and the bats were out flying, darts in the low sky. I could barely see down to the creek, but the cold and the wet came up the hill with a mossy taste. The water was slacking off now, only a hint of snow up the canyon rims.

When we couldn't see anybody but ourselves standing there, I said, "Time to ice?"

"Not tonight," Galen said. "We have to plan your future. It's good to let the heat stretch you out some anyway. A growing boy like you."

I followed him back to his cabin. It was put together with staples and spit, falling in on itself, little more than a fort I would have built when I was a kid. Outside were a number of ragtag boards he'd scavenged from the dump at the Hobel transfer site. We sat on those. In the dark I could barely see him.

"Roll us some beavers and we'll talk about it," Galen said.

And I did. And when I was done with that I made what he called an Indian fire, a smallish blaze in the oil drum he'd sawn in half. He brought out a pot and made soup from the grasses that grew in the pocket meadow behind the cabin. I went through the woods to my camp and retrieved the kokanee I'd seined that day.

We didn't talk while we ate, just thought about the summers to come when I'd be hurling my way up to the show. When we were done I looked up and saw Galen in the orange firelight and he was smiling at me.

"Kit," he said. His voice was gentle and easy. "It's time I showed you some things. About the game." He went back into his cabin and brought out an album.

There were pictures of all sorts in there and pieces cut out of the newspaper that were yellow with brown edges. For a time he leafed through them sitting next to me and his mouth went to form a little whistle and his breathing came through in a sigh.

I looked at the old pictures and the words that were hard to read and after a bit I said, "That's you." I pointed at a ball player in a uniform, sleeves rolled up, two arms as big as Thanksgiving hams. Galen nodded. I touched my finger to it. The man was big, not as big as my daddy, but big. He showed me the team picture, all those fellows standing with legs spread, hands in mitts.

"Uh-huh," he said. He tapped the picture. "The Ely Bombers."

"Number thirteen," I said.

"That's right. Bad luck to any batter who faced me. That's what they called me. 'Bad Luck.'"

"Ely," I said. "Ely." I pushed my hand through knots of hair and tried to dream a picture of it.

Galen said, "Right," and he told me about barnstorming through the Nevada desert. "Played out our string in Fallon, Reno, Ely," he said. "Parts east, too. Utah."

He pointed to a place that was beyond the woods and the Trinities. His voice came across miles of open land. The fire crackled in the drum and it smelled piney and good. Galen went back into the house and came out with some framed pictures. I stirred up a curtain of sparks.

One was a photo of him in his uniform and it was signed. He was a handsome man back then, that 13, not a whisker on him.

There were some other pictures, too. A little tract house. Out on the front steps were him and a lady with brown hair, a girl in a jumper, and one of those yip-yip dogs.

Galen looked at that picture extra hard and his hand got to shaking. "I threw it away," he said, almost a whisper. "Threw it away." His face had that faraway stare, looked as if it would break open. Then he said some words that weren't words at all, only mumbles. I started to tell him different, started to say all the things he'd been to me these past three months.

He waved me off. His voice caught in his throat. "I couldn't get a grip," he said. "I had the life right in my hand and lost it. Pills. I was eating them like candy. After the accident."

I thought then about my daddy and all the pills and drugs they pumped him full of and how he wasn't really my daddy anymore. I thought about the kids in juvie center who did time for using and how they walked around as if they'd been hollowed out, no insides at all.

Galen got up and paced around, his coonskin tail switching.

I was sorry he'd ever taken those pictures out. "Tell me again," I said. "Galen, tell me what it'll be like."

His eyes were wet but he smiled anyway and I hoped in his head he'd walked down that street, away from that tract house, hoped he was back up here with me again.

"Kit," he said. "You'll be the best, bar none. You'll never see a place like Ely except to say good-bye." His hand snapped as if he was throwing an Uncle Charley.

"The truth?" I said. I poked a stick in the fire.

"Sure as I'm here." His bum arm went flapping.

"You're coming, too," I said. "I learned all that I know from you. My bag of pitches."

Galen didn't say anything. Usually when I said that, he'd slap me on the back, tell me to look lively.

I said, "You'll be . . . my personal trainer."

He smiled. "I ain't leaving you, boy," he said and right then I felt warmer than our Indian fire.

"Tell me what it'll be like," I said. "One more time."

And he did. And before he was done I'd fallen asleep. I woke up once during the night and I saw him standing over me, his face stilled and sad looking. And I went back to sleep thinking what a good life it would be, me throwing the ball right by the batters, Galen with me every step of the way, out there, the two of us, riding the asphalt toward a place I couldn't even see clearly in dreams.

GALEN WAS QUIET AFTER the night of looking at the pictures. I thought he was planning my future, which tryout we'd be going to and where. It was almost July. I was out there throwing, going through my bag of pitches. He was behind me but wasn't calling out the situations anymore, just stood there as the pitches came homing in.

"I'm about to chop down that tree with my rocks," I said to him with a laugh. The dogwood blooms were gone, the madrones all peeled off, undertrunks snake green.

"Easy, Kit," he said. "Always save some of it. Don't show them everything you got." It was the first comment Galen had said in twenty minutes. I was all set to go down to the creek and seine for that night's fish if he didn't snap out of it.

Galen walked down by the ponderosa and stood off to the first-base side. "Go on, boy. I'm a live batter." He picked up a stick and held it in his good arm, waggled it. I had to smile: this naked man, maybe fifty, swinging a branch at a kid heaving rocks.

"Come on," he said.

I wound up and let fly. The rock thudded against the trunk.

"All right, Kit. Come inside. I'm crowding the plate."

I threw and he fell back and pointed the branch at me. "You're a pistol, you are," he said. "Those are bullets."

I squinted my eyes tight and imagined those bikini girls sitting in the front row screaming up a storm, the idea of them cheering for me. And Galen was number 13 again.

"Bottom of the ninth," he yelled to me now, a big, loopy grin splitting his face for the first time that day. "Last pitch. Turn up the heat, boy."

I didn't leave anything back when I threw. It was a loud shot, splinters flying everywhere. What I saw after my follow-through was that rock lodged halfway into the meat of the trunk.

Galen was beside himself. "I'd like to see Walter Johnson do that," he said. He started singing a song, an old one I hadn't heard before, something about bright lights and big cities.

I was swinging my arms like windmills when I first heard the woman's voice. I thought it was a telephone ringing through the woods, the way her voice sounded. But then I heard it again. Then a tinkly little voice. And then another.

In all my days up there, we hadn't seen anyone except our two skins. I was shaking because I thought they'd finally come for what I did to Foster Bob. Galen, too, was spooked, his twenty-five years alone looking to be slipping out of his hand just then. He stopped trying to pry the rock out of the ponderosa and ran over to a dogwood in the glade, motioned for me to follow. I climbed up the ladder of branches, hooked my legs over a limb, hung down like a bat, pulled him up into the leaves with me.

Into the clearing walked a woman with two little girls in cute green hiking shorts. "Matthew," she called. One of the little girls said something and she shushed her. "Quiet, Elissa," she said to the dark-haired kid, "he's your brother."

The other kid had light hair. That one said, "Matthew's a poo-poo."

The one named Elissa said, "He's mean as a penis. I want to go back to camp."

The mother hugged her sides as if she was cold even though it was a hot day. She turned as she hugged herself and looked around.

"Look at that tree," the light-haired one said. She went over to the ponderosa. "It's growing a rock."

"It's growing a rock," Elissa said.

"Matthew," the mother called.

They passed right under the dogwood we were hiding in but didn't look up. I got red-faced at the idea of them looking up and seeing Galen hanging down. It occurred to me then how unsettling it was the way he traipsed around, how it could make me feel funny inside. I got a weird picture of what it'd be like when we hit the bigs, me in uniform, Galen, naked with skin the color of bricks.

When I looked over his way I saw his eyes were pooled and dripping. If the three of them down there hadn't moved, if they were still right under us, they might have thought it was raining, he was crying that hard.

After some time, they drifted off through the woods again. I could hear the mother calling, "Matthew," every so often. Hearing it like that, the mother's calling coming through the trees, it gave a sharp, sad feeling, the thought of that missing little boy, even if he was only missing for an hour or two, or was maybe already back at their tent, wondering where his mother and two sisters were. After some minutes we climbed down and I went back through the woods and holed up in my tree sling for the rest of the afternoon and night. I couldn't even think about pitching.

I WAS STILL GROWING all the time. My clothes were riding up. I was going to turn into a giant before I knew it.

I'd picked out a tree in my stretch of woods and paced off sixty feet and threw there to keep me sharp. It wasn't the same as with Galen. But he was walking around those days like he wasn't in these woods, like he was still circling the block where that tract house was.

Meanwhile, I seined for kokanee and browns, caught enough to dry and smoke for jerky. Also I lashed a square frame of oak boughs up in my sling and pulled all the rope tight, which made for bedding that was good as any I'd had.

Galen came waltzing through the woods the first day of July. "Boy howdy," I said. "Look who it is. Old number thirteen. Bad luck himself."

He gave a wave like he was wiping a window with cloth. "July Fourth," he said. "It's your big game. Next stop after that is the bush leagues." He scratched his beard with his hand.

I rolled us two beavers and we smoked. "You're ready as ever. The Hall for sure," he said.

"You think?" I said, tapping the ash.

"I do," he said and he told me we'd simulate a whole game to see what I was made of. "The Fourth," he said. After he left I thought about the possibilities, the very idea that my life could have some kind of plan to it, not just happen like an accident, the very idea.

THE THREE DAYS UNTIL the Fourth went slow as a month. I rested in the sling, ate jerky, thought about batters and pitches and situations.

I didn't see Galen during any of that time, just stayed in my end of the woods. When the day came, it broke hot and blue and I went through the glade. Galen had an old baseball cap on, the one from his days on the Bombers. He didn't say anything, only gave a small nod.

He had a radio in his hand and he fiddled with it until the static went away. Then a voice came in clear and I heard what it was—the parade down in Weaverville. There was a drum going and the announcer talking and trumpets also. Then it got hushed and what I heard took me back over ten years, the bells coming over the radio. All the kids in Weaverville did it, ring the bells for independence on the Fourth.

What I thought of then wasn't pitches or situations but the time I did it myself so long ago, ring the bells for freedom, and I could see my daddy above the crowd, the biggest man in the county. I remembered how he told me I was the best ringer there was. "A dead ringer, Kit," he'd said to me afterward as I sucked on a bottle of soda. "I stood taller," he said, "because I knew I was your dad."

When the last bell stopped ringing, they played the anthem and Galen took off his hat, put it over his heart, and I did the salute I learned in juvie center.

"Play ball," Galen said when it was over and we did.

I was on fire. I struck out the side the first inning. The players kept going down, couldn't hit me with a plywood board.

Galen ran all over the field in his hat. He tied up his beard with a rubber band and announced every pitch, every time the batter stepped out of the box. The rocks went on a rope from my hand to the ponderosa.

Hours after we'd started, Galen said, "Ninth inning. Bottom. Game on the line." He held up his hand to call time to the umpire, came trotting out to me.

"I had five pitches," he said.

"You only told me four. Only four pitches."

"I had five."

I twiddled the rock in my hand. It was a tense thing standing there, game on the line.

Galen was breathing hard. "I had five. Kylertown Trolley. A pitch of my own invention. Nasty bit of work." He took my hand, showed me the grip. My fingers looked to be spider legs holding the rock. "You twist when you release." He showed me. He looked over to where the umpire was. "Let's go," he said.

"But the game's on the line."

"Throw it," he said. His blue eyes were dark as night water. "Throw it."

And I did. A full inning of Kylertown Trolleys. The pitch worked like magic, ran to the left and tailed back to the right, a crazy, impossible movement. Galen hopped up and down, laughed like a coot. And when the inning was done he mobbed me up there on the mound, pulled me in close, said in my ear, "You can write your own ticket now, son. You belong to the world, is what." And then he went running into his shack.

He came back with the framed pictures under his arm, all those old photos of the tract house and him in his uniform. He propped them up, one by one, by the ponderosa. "Go ahead," he said.

I threw pitch after pitch at the tree, each one more perfect than the next. The glass flew into little triangles and sounded like the bells coming over the radio again, the glass tinkling like that.

Galen, he had a real easy look on his face. He kind of hummed to himself the whole time while I made a mess of rocks and glass and frames.

Night was rolling in by the time I'd fractured the last of the photos. We stood facing the other across the length of home and the mound and didn't say anything. It was a warm night and the flies were out in numbers. I could smell the pines and the sharpness of the madrones, their leaves coming down like spring rain.

Seeing him across that distance, I knew then that I'd been through something. I didn't even see the clouds come in when they did. But the first bass note of thunder uprooted me from the spot. Rain came down big as eggs and the lightning came in and thunder banged and shook the trees. In one of the flashes I saw Galen's eyes larger than dinner plates, saw the twenty-five years of what his life had been. That was before my daddy was sick, before he was my daddy even.

A bolt came down and exploded in my end of the woods and I ran through the grove, waving back to Galen as I did. The strike had hit high above my tree sling, making a snag of the topmost part of the hanging madrone. Way up there I could see the fire and embers glowing. After the rain stopped I watched the red flames go to black and I thought this was how I wanted it to be for me. I wanted to blaze across the sky and leave a trail of fire so everybody could know I'd been there.

THE NEXT DAY I woke up to bits of madrone everywhere. My arm was sore from pitching and I went down to the creek to soak it. Once that was done, I decided to go over and see Galen, relive yesterday's glory.

When I came through the woods I saw more things heaped down by the ponderosa. His clippings album was torn this way and that, the pictures of Galen wadded up and wet from rain. Other stuff was there, too, postcards and game programs and clothing, stuff he'd never shown me, pieces of his life from before.

I whistled and hallooed through the trees for him, went down to the stream and kicked through the shallows, watched the gold flecks in the side pools.

It was up at the cabin that I knew he'd cleared out. The place was scoured empty, his kit gone. I went by the ponderosa and threw some rocks. The magic from yesterday had disappeared, though. I tried every pitch in the bag, every last one, but I was just a sixteen-year-old kid again who'd never go anywhere on account of my pitching.

I looked up at the Douglas fir and almost expected to see the spurs gone but they were still there; only that missing arm had loosed its grip. I rolled myself one last beaver before lighting out to the next place that would have me. Before I smoked it, I went out to the ponderosa. I threw that fluky fifth pitch, the Kylertown Trolley. It moved like something I'd never seen before, as if God alone was pushing it. And I swear, at that very moment, the river, it sounded just like applause.

Darkness Runs

Darkness runs in Quimby like a horse. He spins his stories in a voice that's husky as evening, sits before my desk at the Nor El Muk Clinic these early spring days. Outside the window the season hasn't yet alighted in the trees and the winter snows still grip the shoulders of Hayfork Bally.

"It's where all the garbage of the river washes up," Tucker had said back when he called two weeks ago from Sierra Pacific to tell me about Quimby's encampment. "He's got some little girl there. Running around naked as Pocahontas she is."

I'd asked Frankie Sykes about the narrow flat between the canyons after the call, the place Tucker had described. Frankie, a Nomlaki, stared at the bulletin board in the hallway outside my office. He pressed pushpins into the cork and chewed the inside of his cheek as though it were gum.

We'd been arguing about the clinic lately, what was left of it. The staff was skinned down to a skeleton crew of just the two of us. A dying animal, Frankie had started calling it.

"*Loq caraw* is the Wintu name for that place," he'd finally said.

"A special place." He knew who Quimby was, too. "He's a born-in-the-woods, a *tintailtcwen*," Frankie said and later explained to me what a bride-price was, the shame that was Quimby's mother, marrying an outcast, a slave who was no more than spit or dung. He waved me forward as he explained. I followed his trail of words, Frankie going slowly, always waiting for me to catch up. "Dogs," he'd said. "Filthy dogs that'll fuck anything. Brother, sister, mother. It doesn't matter. They're not people, *tintailtcwen*, can't live or even set foot inside the village. Me, I'd stick with helping the people."

But still. I wasn't prepared for what I found after five miles of rutted trail. They had a fire going on the river rocks, the smoke from it a snake in the morning sky. East Fork was running heavy, the melt and March rains spilling over the banks, leaving a deep tarn in the flat.

And there was Katy. A little girl with sprung ribs at water's edge working on a red lolly. She was five or six years old, acorn dark and naked. Bruises like squashed plums ran up her legs and covered her belly and bottom.

She skittered off into the trees. In front of me Quimby's scabby Chevy was heeled over, the camper shell pulled off of it and ditched on the rocks. A cooler bobbed in the pool, lashed to a boulder. Bottles, bones, plastic bags, tin cans everywhere. A line of human waste curved like a sickle near the manzanita where the trail opened into the clearing.

"Hello," I called. Nothing. The door to the camper shell was propped open, the edge of a sleeping bag poking out. I heard clicking noises coming from inside and bent down to look in. What I saw was Quimby, hulling hazelnuts, his eyes shining.

"Pretty soon the suckerfish and riffle pikes," he said and smiled. "The *kuwa*," he said.

We talked like that, me kneeling at the mouth of the shell, Quimby on top of the sleeping mat inside. He gave off a musk of sweat, urine, wood smoke.

He told me of the fish weir the people built across the Trinity at Hoopa when he was a boy. "The water, it was an angry bird's wings," he said, showing me with his hands how the spawning salmon held the current from passing through the dam's lattice-work, the fish beating the water, the weir creaking under the weight.

"Beyond your northward arm," he said and waved at the sugar pines on the other side of the tarn. He described how his father used the juice for medicine, never mentioning his name, the utter-ance of it apparently a sin even for a *tintailtcwen*. He spoke of someone he called Sister, who had moved on to the Pit-McCloud, to the Wenemem.

"Is she your sister, too?" I said, pointing at the trees where the girl had run.

He stared at me, said nothing.

"Was Sister her mother?"

The wind blew down off Hayfork Bally and cupped the surface of the water.

I said, "This isn't right. You can't stay here."

"It is *loq caraw*."

"I know. But it's also Sierra Pacific's."

"They can have the trees," Quimby said.

"There will be people coming in the next few days." I explained about the social workers.

The team came two days later at six A.M. The girl couldn't or didn't talk, it turned out, fought like a wolf, biting Darcy right through her field coat; the workers called her Katy because she chittered away like a katydid in the back of the jeep. They brought her down to the clinic to get cleaned up, then placed her in a temporary foster home, the Gilmore farm in Big Bar, until we could decide what to do with her.

Noon the same day the team went back to the clearing to roust Quimby, told him I was to be his counselor. The storm that had been gathering all morning, funneled through the Hayfork Divide, spilling drops the size of pebbles. He was sitting on a boulder by the pool, no shirt on, rain soaking his face.

A week later he came to the clinic. I heard he was living in his Chevy now off Dog Run Creek. He walked into my office smelling of wood smoke.

"I need to ask you some questions," I said.

"You are one of the people?" he said.

"I'm part."

"What part?" His skin was like oxblood, his hair long and black and stringy as a horse's tail.

"My grandmother," I said.

"You are a city Indian, then."

Quimby told me more about the people—the Chimarikos, Achomawis, Yukis—about Sister's puberty dance. "It was the year of her *hisi*," he said, pointing down below his belt, "the time of her first moon-sickness. She rose early that morning, stripped a maple bark apron. The rest of the women got up early, too."

His voice worked like a drug; once inside me I couldn't get it out. "Sister stuck her little finger with a splinter," Quimby said. "She wiped the blood on dead leaves and traveled downhill to the north to the brush shelter and ate nothing but acorn soup."

Frankie Sykes was pushing a broom outside my office. He pulled faces at me on the other side of the glass door, but I was in the brush shelter with Sister. Quimby said, "She lived alone there for a month. For the first five days she stayed awake with the rib of a red fox to ward off bad dreams."

He told me more about "the one who came before," his father. When Quimby was sixteen his father fell down in the street in Helena, laughed and froze himself to death. The Loknorharas, the white people in town, said he looked just like a cigar store Indian.

At the burial his father was swaddled in bearskin. They wrapped him with string and money. The grave was undercut toward the west and they prodded the body into the cavity with rods.

It went on this way, the stories. When Quimby was done, we watched each other.

"I need you to sign some papers," I said eventually.

"I cannot sign my name," he said. "How do you sign your name, how can anyone? It's like drawing on water."

Frankie's long face was in the glass behind Quimby, lips tight. He shook his head, hands going back and forth like a referee, one above the other.

"You can't read," I said.

Quimby said, "Words aren't real." He moved in his seat, the vinyl complaining underneath him. "They don't tell any story."

"This is your case," I said, holding up the file. "These words that aren't real to you do tell your story. There are regulations in here, too. They say I need to see you twice a week." I marked Tuesday and Thursday in my Sierra calendar. "Do you understand?" I said, "Tuesday and Thursday," and showed him the calendar.

Quimby nodded and stared at the photo of a coyote barking that was snapped in Kalispell, Montana.

The whole of our time together he didn't ask once about Katy. Frankie leaned against the doorjamb of my office after Quimby left, blocking my way. He said, "If I was you, I wouldn't believe that fucker for a minute. Not one." And he looked at me as if it was something he couldn't put in words, something I would never understand.

I DO NOT WALK with the Wintu, Chimariko, Shasta, Achomawi, Nomlaki, or Hupa. What little people blood runs in me is Ohlone, the people who walked the land that is now the Bay Area.

It's blood that runs thin: my hair is light brown, almost blond; my skin only red when sunburnt.

My grandmother, a full-blood Ohlone, was always Nana to me, never the name the people have, *putacepet*. I was thirteen when I found out what she was, a distinction I wore among my friends like a badge, a time of Indian beads and hemp clothes and ceremonial feathers.

But when the fashion faded, my grandmother returned in my eyes to the woman who played mah-jongg weekly, knitted ski sweaters for me, watched *The Match Game* every day on TV.

And yet. On the edge of dreams I kept thinking I heard more, something wild, but when I awoke all I heard was foghorns lowing in the night.

In college I minored in psychology and parsed my dreams with the help of Freud and Jung. By the time of graduation I thought I knew who I was, the neat, straight explanations true as a knife edge. Even so, every now and then I still felt the pull of something that landed softly as a bird, smelled of trees and fish and air, then flew back away.

A dozen years later, after my marriage to a white woman splintered, I traveled north and earned a master's in social work at Humboldt State. After graduation, I followed 299 east, chasing the steelhead upstream to the Trinities, where I fished. When summer faded and the Alaska cold fronts started to blow in and the steelhead thinned out, I stayed on. I read books in the Hayfork Public Library evenings, hiked the trails during the day.

It's a green world up here, only a few asphalt roads worming through the Trinities, only a handful of towns taking root under the old growth forest. The story of this land is still written on the hills and it dates back to when the people walked the land, a story so big and untamable it still resists retelling by Loknorharas, outsiders.

One day in October I saw the hiring notice for the director of the Nor El Muk Clinic on the library's bulletin board and phoned the listed number. Two days later I drove to the California Indian Policy office in Redding for the interview, my freshly typed résumé on the seat next to me in my beater VW. The following week word was left for me at Tom's Small Fry, where I ate every night after the rivers were fished out, that the job was mine.

I met Frankie shortly after. He was my last interview for the day, had a mustache then that was only a rumor on his upper lip. His hair was pulled back into a ponytail that was already graying. Traditional calibration tattoos ran up his arms.

"So you're a cowboy playing Indian," he said when I told him the plans of the clinic. And I saw then he was exactly what I needed: an Indian guide, one of the people; he knew this country and could take me to the heart of it. I offered him the job as my assistant on the spot.

Over beers at Mountain Mama's he said, "Getting money for these people is going to be about as easy as catching a bird with a butterfly net, you know."

I knew. The people in Redding had told me these hills were dotted with tribes and clans but none had federal recognition; funding would be a constant problem.

On the third round Frankie squeezed his eyes closed, as if taking aim on me. I watched him pour the rest of his beer.

"What," he said, "you think every Indian can't handle the sauce? Three's my limit." He pulled the hair up on his head. "My wife scalps me if I have more than three. I don't know how she knows, but she does. *Qiloqsas*, the people call it, scalping."

"I'm part Indian," I said and told him of Nana.

"That's a nice story," he said. "Tell you what, if you could put that in a bottle, you could market it."

I DISAPPEAR INTO QUIMBY'S stories.

I should know better. My job: I'm supposed to counsel him, help him secure a place to live, check his medical condition, see if anybody needs an extra hand—setting choker cables for Sierra Pacific, maybe, pushing a broom on the duckpin alleys in Forest Glen, anything.

Word has it he's still got a camp out on Dog Run Creek. I hear he's digging trenches for culverts up north on 3 one day, pouring concrete for McCully Construction over in Del Loma another. Frankie says he's busking for nickels, dimes, and quarters in the parking lot of the Midway Mart some nights. I can't say for certain. Quimby and I don't talk about that. It's not that I don't mean to because I do. Every time before his appointment his folder is open on my desk in front of me, the words spelling out what's supposed to be done, what has to be.

But then he comes into my office. He smells of the brown trout he caught and fried up that morning. His hands are stained from elderberries and grouse berries. With him there in the office, I know what it is that unhinges me. He's an archaeological find, not only bones, but flesh. It's as if he stepped right out of a history book, out of somewhere deep inside me.

Today I'm writing in my calendar as Quimby comes into the office.

"Words," he says and smiles at me. "Words cannot tell you anything. You cannot see a tree in a word. No, no, please continue. Let me see you make your words."

I write *report due for BIA* in the date box for Wednesday and Quimby watches. When I'm done he's bent over me and I think for a moment he's reading what I've written but then remember most Wintu can't read. He's studying this week's wildlife photo in my Sierra calendar: a lodgepole pine in Yellowstone throwing shadows on snow.

He says, "This can tell you something." His thumb leaves a greasy smudge on the snowdrift in the photo and he walks around the desk to the chair across from me and sits. "I've seen snow like this," he says and points out the window. The sun is partly covered by clouds. "Up on Weaver Bally," he says.

"Yes," I say. "I've been there."

"To Snow Lake?" he asks.

I say nothing.

"Long ago it was called Snow Mountain," he says. "There was water there, water frozen deep with snow. 'You will be Snow Lake,' God said."

Quimby's voice sighs, like wind. His hands and arms form a blunt steeple, describing the mountain. One hand scoops out the slope, where Snow Lake was.

He says, "Beyond the lake water flowed down from a canyon. This was where many people gathered, *baqi nomwaqin*."

He sits back in the chair, eyes pressing shut, barrel chest swelling like a bellows. He takes up the story's melody again. "In that time, the people were animals. Bear, panther, deer, coyote, raccoon, badger, and beaver. That is where they met. All stood ready to fight. The birds sang 'wene hene ya,' the stellar jay, scrub-jay, and towhee. Then the north ridge fought with arrows they made from pebbles. The south ridge used slingshots. Many were killed and the fighting lasted days. 'We will be wiped out,' the animals of the north ridge said finally. 'Let's run,' they said. And they did. Then the south ridge made fire and danced and sang 'wene hene ya.'"

Quimby watches the white oak outside the window. He pulls at his shirt that's little more than a knot of flannel. Seeing him there, I don't quite know what kind of animal he is, only know it's a breed that exists somewhere between town and the wild.

I wait minutes for his voice to pour through me once more. The only sound is birds twittering outside.

"Soon after the victory, the animals from the south ridge drank the water of Snow Lake and died. When there were only enough to count on hands"—Quimby holds up both palms, wiggles his twisted fingers—"when there are only so many left, God said, 'There will be no more fighting among the animals and no more Snow Lake,' and He drained the lake. God said, 'I will leave only the snow and the bones and the rocks and arrows so that people can remember.'"

Quimby smiles at me, his arms and hands forming the hill again. "I still see the snow and the water-washed rocks and bones at this place of the *sawal* where the animals met and fought. I remember." He stands up from the chair, says, "The snow, it can tell you something," and leaves.

I look at the smudged photo in the calendar after he's gone, think of Katy at the Gilmore farm in Big Bar. She's still not talking. At least she's safe from Quimby now. From all reports, she's a little animal girl herself, a hair-pulling, holy terror with the other foster children and the barn animals. Edna Gilmore tells me this when she calls, Katy going after the other kids, going after the sheep, goats, and ponies.

THE CLINIC IS A bird losing its feathers, each week another feather. Two weeks ago it was the funding for outpatient renal treatment; last week cutbacks on the staff of visiting RNs and paring back the days we're open to Tuesday, Wednesday, Thursday; this week it's eliminating alcohol and substance abuse counseling. In a little while we will not be able to fly at all, the only clinic for the people on this side of the mountains.

There's still the Redding Rancheria Satellite Clinic, but that's a long way to travel—two hours over alpine roads that spool through Buckhorn Summit, drop down and flatten out across Whiskeytown Lake, climb again through Shasta, and finally empty into town. It's an icy bobsled run during winter. Summers, the blacktop's hot as a kiln. The Bureau of Indian Affairs tells me the Redding Rancheria is more than adequate for regional needs. But Weaverville is the farthest most Wintu have ever traveled. For them, Redding is a black growth beyond the east horizon.

Still, we continue to flap our wings. Frankie and I petition the offices in Washington. We file reports, write council members of federally recognized tribes. We call in every marker we have.

All of our little noise convinces the Advisory Council on California Indian Policy to grant a stay of execution. They give us a chance to plead our case in a meeting that's eight days from now. We open earlier and close later on the three days the clinic still operates, arranging treatment for ankle sprains and the croup, placing people in jobs. The other days we work until we drop. Outside the season is exploding—white dogwood blooms, ceonothus covering the hills like purple wildfire, oak leaves outside my window fanning open. We work so hard, we barely see it.

Lunches we've taken to going out to the Frontier Kitchen, something we've never done. Before we always brown-bagged it and ate by ourselves. But this is ceremony, we understand, a last supper stretching over a week of noontime hours.

Between nibbling down fries at the Frontier today, Frankie says, "At least we finally got that cat piss smell out of the place before the doors close." I remember the two of us scrubbing and scrubbing out the rooms of the boarded-up veterinary hospital before the clinic opened. We worked seven days a week to ready the ramshackle L-shaped building on the corner lot. It rained all that winter and every time it did, something animal breathed out of the walls and linoleum. It didn't matter. The people flocked to the clinic that winter and after, up to two hundred cases a month.

"I saw Katy yesterday," I say and tell Frankie of my visit to the Gilmore farm. Someone back in the kitchen yells and the swinging doors slam open and Frankie's chewing slows when I describe the scene. Katy had on a jumper several sizes too large, had scuffed Mary Janes on her feet. There were trails of urine running down her legs with dirt stuck where it had dried. The Gilmores had strapped a football helmet on her and she was bashing the fence post with the top of her head like a hammer hitting a nail over and over again. The goats rolled their eyes back in their sockets, crowded against one another in the far corner. I say, "The Gilmores are doing everything they can but she's too much," and I think of the look in her eyes, black and feral. I say, "She's disrupting the whole place. They're going to have to send her to Redding. They've already put in the call."

"She's trouble, kemo sabe," Frankie says and works on his burger. His face closes up, annoyed, mouth working like pistons. He's someplace just this side of exasperation.

I say, "Quimby never asks after her. Not once. Not how she is, where she is. Nothing. I don't get it." I tell Frankie of this morning's visit, about the story Quimby told me, the children of the woods, *hotoy ilawih*.

What I don't tell him is how Quimby's voice works on me like dope. Even in the daylight of my office I can never seem to see all of him. After he leaves only his smell stays with me, never his image.

When he told the story to me today, I closed my eyes and his face and the walls to my office faded and I was on the bluff he described near Canyon Creek, *tusono*, the place coarse with shale. I was walking with two hunting Wintu and we heard the sound of many children talking in the mountains and laughing. They played and made the dust fly up. The hunting Wintu and I sneaked behind the bushes. What we saw was only one, uphill north he came. He was a boy who looked just like an old man, had the face of an old man and stood stooped. What we heard was the voices of many talking and laughing, but there was just the one. The next day we returned to this place, *tusono*. But there was no one there, no more children of the woods, just the shale, the canyon, and the bluff. The boy was gone.

When I'm done, Frankie says, "I know that story, heard it when I was a kid. *Hotoy ilawih*." He runs an onion ring around the ketchup on his plate. "You'd think he was a shaman, the way he talks. He's a dog, *tintailtcwen*."

Frankie looks at me as if he's eaten bad meat but tells the waitress everything's just fine when she comes by to check on us and orders himself another Coke. We talk awhile about the meeting in Redding coming up next Friday, about what's left to do for the report, and work out a schedule for who gets the clinic's only computer. After he drains the Coke, Frankie turns around in his seat, looking for the waitress and the bill. When he turns back, he says to me, "I know you. You think this one can make up for everything else. It can't. Forget him."

Later in the car, he props his feet up on the dashboard as I drive and says, "You want stories, I can tell you stories," but he doesn't tell me any. He says, "You don't know what you're playing with there," and holds up both his hands, shakes his head at me. This, our quiet war over the *tintailtcwen*, is the first time in our four years of working together that I take a different path than he, my guide, suggests.

QUIMBY IS IN MY dreams.

Today, Tuesday, he came into my office, watched me draw circles around Frankie's notation *Redding meeting 1:30* in the Friday space. He looked long and hard at the photo of a bald eagle alighting on a tree in the Chilkat Preserve.

I said, "Alaska."

"The north," he said.

Asleep in bed I saw the story he told me earlier. An old man and his daughter living all alone. One from the north comes and falls in love with the girl, begs the father to let him take her back north with him. The father fears she will freeze to death and forbids it. But the young man does not heed the old man's words and steals the girl away in a night of no moon. He marries the girl and they cross the land toward the north, to *temeha*, the land of cold. They live there a long, long time. The man's family loves the girl. "Such a pretty one," they say. "We will all take care of her." They build a house in the snow and live there a long time.

"It is the way that God determined it," Quimby said.

THERE IS NO TIME to drive to the Gilmores to visit Katy today.

Our meeting with the Advisory Council on California Indian Policy is tomorrow; there is still too much work to be done on the report. Frankie stayed all last night and through the morning running spreadsheets.

When I come in today, he's asleep on a gurney in the hallway. In the sharp morning light, dust covers everything like fur—the floor, the walls, the gurney, even Frankie. I bring a blanket out from one of the examination rooms to cover him.

Later after he wakes, he comes into my office, eyes red, hair falling loosely and not tied back in the usual ponytail. "It is a good day to die," he says, lifts the computer up from my desk, and walks back out.

I get the call from Edna Gilmore a little after nine. Her voice is a siren. What I hear is breakfast, fork, goat, that girl. Then Edna sobbing, her breaths coming in hiccups and gulps. Someone is yelling behind her; it must be her husband, Lester. I hear children keening in notes that climb straight off the scale, Lester yelling, trying to quiet them. I promise to drive out immediately.

When I yell to Frankie to tell him where I'm headed, he calls back, "What did I tell you?"

It's like a spell driving to the Gilmores, everything slow and elastic. I'm punching the accelerator flat, doing seventy-five on the dead stretches, cutting the yellow dashed line where the road gets squirrelly, coming in and out of the sun. The trunks of the roadside pines and firs and spruces click by like pickets in a fence.

Even before I get to the gate of the farm, I can see figures, small, the size of ants, running across the pasture. Here, out of the shade, sunlight bleaches everything.

Edna is waiting for me when I pull in where the gravel driveway circles in front of the farmhouse. She's in her housecoat and her thin legs are speckled with paint the color of wine.

I still can't make out what she's saying. Her round cheeks are shiny with tears, her chin and lips trembling. She pulls me toward the barn. The screen door slams on the house, a boy about twelve years old sprints out, screaming, and Lester comes out from inside, catches him up, carries him back inside.

And there's Katy outside the goat pen, tethered to a post.

She's wearing the same too-large jumper. It's no longer light blue, and when I see the baby goat, I know it's not paint on Edna's legs. I take the fork that's still in Katy's hands. The blood is everywhere.

The goat. The fork has been raked up and down the goat's flanks and has punctured both eyeballs. The skin is pulled back along its belly and something white and red peeks through, intestines probably. Its tongue is pulled out of its mouth. There's a blast from a shotgun along its head and the smell of cordite—that's from Lester, I find out later, from when he first came outside during breakfast to look for Katy. What he found was the goat running blind and he ran to the locked cabinet in the barn and returned with his shotgun.

The other goats in the pen run crazy now, around and around and around like water going down a drain. Saliva hangs from their mouths in threads; they kick at one another and run, blood spraying from their legs. In the middle a single goat is bawling, the dam, its teats swinging, still heavy with milk.

"Call the doctor," I tell Edna. She goes and I untie Katy and strip the jumper off her, just the two of us here now. I hose her down with water and run my fingers in hair stiff as broom bristles and peel the dry blood off. When I go to turn off the spigot, she moves toward the pen, her hands reaching for the goats once more. I grab her before she can slide under the fence slat. I shake her hard, do it again, her head snapping back on her neck, whipping forward, back, forward. I keep on until I see the mark of my hand rising in a red welt on Katy's arm, feel tiny bones under skin. And I hug her to me, hold her fast until the doctor comes, cradling and rocking her, my chin on the top of her head. The doctor gives her something so she'll sleep, stabs her in the hip with the needle and she bares her dirty teeth at me.

After Katy drops off the arrangements are made. I think of the unfinished report still open on my desk for tomorrow's big meeting when I make the phone calls. The people at the home for autistic kids in Redding say they can take Katy on Monday, to keep her sedated until then. I tell this to Edna and Lester. I call Frankie and tell him what's happened.

"So who ever called us noble savages?" he says. "I tell you, this is what I'll really miss about this job." He asks when I think I'll get back.

"I have to go home first. Get a change of clothes."

"He was here," Frankie says, "rooting around your office."

"Right," I say, remembering. "Our Thursday meeting. He likes to read the pictures in my Sierra calendar." On the drive back my soaked jeans are heavy as armor. I wonder which photos Quimby was looking at—thunderstorm over Sedona, saw-whet owls in Whitman National Forest, a giant sequoia—wonder what they told him. His smell comes back to me and fills my car.

THE BIG FRIDAY MEETING turns out to be no meeting at all. In the car we don't talk about what happened out at the Gilmores' yesterday; we hardly talk as we ride into battle. Frankie's wearing a tie. His suit coat rides up short above his wrists and his arms stick out like three-inch pipes.

The further east we go, out of the mountains and closer to town, the more summer is eating into spring. The sun's a blood orange, the brush already going from green to gold to even brown in some spots. After Oak Bottom the road pulls straight and just beyond the turnoff for French Gulch we see pleasure boaters already out on Whiskeytown Lake.

Once we get to the Advisory Council office, there's just a lone secretary eating a ham sandwich at her desk. We tell her who we are.

"I'm sorry," she says after looking in the appointment book, "there must be a mistake. There's no meeting scheduled for today. They're all off-site for the afternoon." She looks the two of us over. "I'll make some calls for you," she says.

We sit. Frankie rolls himself a cigarette and goes outside to smoke. Even with the prints on the wall, sepia-colored old photos of the people, Frankie seems out of place here in town, as if he's from an old Saturday kiddie matinee but in poorly fitting clothes instead of buckskin. I fan myself with our report, take off my coat, roll up my sleeves.

"Nobody knows about any meeting," the secretary says.

I look outside at Frankie blowing smoke rings. "If it's all right with you," I say, "we'll wait." And we do. After the first hour, Frankie doesn't go outside to smoke anymore.

"This is a no-smoking office," she says but Frankie doesn't budge, continues to blow his smoke rings, cigarette after cigarette.

At four-thirty we decide to finally hand the secretary the report and leave. Frankie says as we get in the car, "This makes it official. The red man is code blue in Trinity County."

As we drive back, the thermals climb out of the valley with us, the heat suffocating, more boaters on Whiskeytown Lake now. By the time we finally reach Weaverville, our mouths are dusty, so we go to the Big Foot for a drink.

We start on beer and don't stop after Frankie's limit of three, then begin chasing mescal. After a few of those, the whisky's chasing us.

"To Crazy Horse," Frankie says, downs the mescal, chews on the worm section in his shot glass.

"To Ishi," I say. We kill time toasting every Indian we can think of. Bloody Knife. Sitting Bull. Chief Gall. Black Oak. Iron Hawk. Wooden Leg. Young Hawk. Red Cloud. White Bull.

When we run out of Indians, we start in on tribes: Pomo, Miwok, Yana, Konkow, Lassik, Karuk, Yurok, Tsnungwe, Wiyot. The whisky's a fire inside me. Frankie is talking but I can no longer listen to him. His words wheel around me. I see the smoke rising from his cigarette and I think of shale dust. The lights dim—a brownout at the substation—and what I hear in the dark bar is all the voices of the Big Foot and it sounds like growling in my ears.

Then it's closing time. I drive to Hayfork so slow it's as if I'm tracking someone on a trail. "I don't know where you live," I say to Frankie.

He says, "How long we been working together?" One of his eyes is shut, as if he's winking at me, and he tells me the way. He has a family, I remember, but we've never really talked about them; two boys, I think. I can't even remember his wife's name, only remember he went off to call her sometime during the evening.

"Here," he says when we reach the house. There's a dim light going somewhere inside. On the front porch a child's sled leans against the wall next to the door. It's cedar-shingled, the house, and I think of the old photos of maple Hupa houses with circular door-ways, but his looks nothing like it.

After Frankie gets out, he comes around to my window, bends down. I can smell the mescal and beer.

"We are two sorry shit-faced braves," he says. "I guess you're a full-blood now, a *tomleh* of the people," he says and goes up his front walk, waves at me as he heads into the house. His hand seems to push me away, back toward the road.

IT'S MORNING WHEN I find out Katy is gone. The phone wakes me, splits the hangover that sits low and heavy on my brow, a thunderhead. It's Edna Gilmore. She tells me.

"There are messages everywhere for you," she says. "I called the clinic, your house." The red light on the answering machine blinks at me. "It happened around three yesterday afternoon. He must have climbed up on a ladder. We found it lying against the house. She was sleeping. The pills," Edna says.

We talk about it more. "We weren't equipped to handle her. I did my best," she says.

"I know you did, Edna. You couldn't have done any better."

When I get off I call Frankie. He sounds pinched from all the whisky we drank last night.

He says, "What did I tell you? *Tintailtcwen.* You know, he was poking around in your office when you were up at the farm Thursday with all that goddamn goat business."

"He couldn't read," I say. "That's what he told me."

"Fucking coyote," Frankie says.

Then there is nothing more to say and I get dressed, drive out to Dog Run Creek, its bumpy trail slapping my headache around. After miles of red-clay washboards I find a clearing on the trail along a flat section of the East Fork. The water is running thinner now. The river is a blue scar cut into the sugar pines and blackcaps and scrub oaks. There's garbage on the skirt of gravel bar that bands the water. I kick through it: empty tins of tuna, Ziploc bags, wadded paper, old newspapers, crushed cookie cartons.

Upriver I see a bone, recall a story Quimby had told me. It happened long ago. A bone landed from somewhere far away. The wind blew, the earth shook, the rivers dried up, and all the animals went away, the pronghorn elk, grizzlies, black bears, raccoon, skunks, beavers, all of them. "This bone, this *saxuke*, came from a whirlwind," Quimby said. "God made it happen. It can happen again."

What I see now is Barker Mountain in front of me, green and brown except for the sections blackened by the wildfire that happened several seasons back. Somewhere in the northern edge of the sky I think I see something very, very old. But when I look again, it's nothing. All I see is a flock of birds and wind in the trees.

Smoke

IT WAS TWO DAYS since Massey had tied up the kid. He was trussed up like a Christmas turkey, strapped to a chair in Massey's banged-to shack outside Lemonade Spring.

Massey'd heard him in the clearing. He'd been napping, dreaming of hoisting himself up, out of his woods and the Trinities, into the night sky, the moon maiden glowing in the heavens like the mantle in his propane lantern.

Then he woke. He listened to the swishing of leaves in the garden, was now sure a deer had come out from the forest to nibble the marijuana plants, and he grabbed his sawed-off shotgun, filled it with rock salt, thinking he'd scare the deer away, give it something to think about and remember, and he walked out behind the line of sugar pines quiet as could be.

What Massey saw was the kid kneeling in his magic patch, snipping the plants, a daypack open on the ground. The kid was so caught up in his pruning, probably wondering how the leaves had turned all those Technicolor shades, he never heard anything else.

Massey put the barrel of the sawed-off behind his ear. "Halt," he said. "Who goes there?"

The kid jumped like he was hooked up to electricity.

Massey said, "You're supposed to say, 'It's only me.'" He pushed the muzzle in the kid's back. "That's what you say after I say, 'Halt. Who goes there?'"

"It's only me," the kid said.

"Good," Massey said. "Good. Could use a little more oomph, but okay." He considered what to do next. In all his years up here, Massey had never had any unexpected visitors. This was untracked country, a place only worth getting lost in. Just his partner Zero and his old girlfriend Gail knew the way, maybe not even Gail anymore; she'd deserted him, found her way out of the woods three years ago.

He hoped the kid wouldn't make a move for it. The rock salt would knock him flat and probably out. Either way there'd be the question of what to do with the boy. Massey knew that he wasn't much good with all the shadings involved in a tricky question like that.

He was kneeling in the red dirt, the kid, looking straight ahead trying to take it all in—the marijuana leaves, which were impossible shades of red, blue, yellow, and purple; Massey's shack, which he saw now across the way, its tangle of cast-off boards, tarpaper, nails; the quarter-acre mountain meadow, which was a halo of baldness in the evergreen, oak, and fir forest; the sawed-off barrel sticking in his back.

"What is this?" the kid said finally.

"What is this?" Massey said. He felt a jangly fear, didn't know what to do next. He knew what Zero would say to do, but Zero was miles away in Mad River. Besides, Zero wasn't his boss.

There was also a goosey excitement. It was a difficult thing not to clap the kid on the back, welcome him, difficult, too, to keep the gun fixed on him.

"What is this?" Massey said. "The Three Billy Goats Gruff." He said, "The goats cross the bridge because they want to eat the grass on the other side. That's the grass." He shook one of the rainbow leaves. "There's a big, ugly troll, too. That's me." He traced outlines with the muzzle tip on the kid's shirt. "What say you turn around nice and slow."

The kid turned in the dirt on his knees, looked up, his brown eyes squinty from the sun, which was sitting on Massey's right shoulder like a second head. And when he turned, Massey saw it. The kid looked like a younger version of Zero: the same hair, which was black-bear black, hair finer than thread and falling down straight, then curling over both ears like muffs; he was rangy like Zero, too, except without the gut, a little young for that yet. The tennis shirt, Bean walking shorts, and hiking boots were all wrong. But the rest of him was Zero.

The kid was gulping, looking up at Massey. Here, in the thick of the Trinity National Forest, in this mountain meadow not on any map, miles from anyone and anything, Massey must have seemed like some kind of god that had dropped out of the trees. He hoped his size was enough to keep the kid in line. He was six foot four, had a chest more rounded than the hull of a rowboat, and he puffed himself up to all of it. Even though the gun was only packed with rock salt, he wasn't sure he could squeeze the trigger.

"Who else is with you?" Massey said.

"It's only me."

"Improvise, kid." He cocked the hammer of the sawed-off just for show. "You've used that line already."

"Fishing," the kid said in a skinny voice. He cleared out his throat, told Massey his business up here was fishing.

"I get it," Massey said. "You catch them with just your hands. Very sporting."

The kid looked down at his hands and back up into Massey's face. He gave him one of Zero's smirky looks. "If you're the troll," he said, "where's your bridge?"

Massey laughed. "Spunk," he said and saw the kid was only putting up a good front, was in truth bullyragged, more fidgety and jumpy than a cat. "I like that. I'm laughing with you." He nodded at him. "The bridge? Too many damn goats," he said. "I get to thinking, Fuck that shit. The noise. *Trip-trap-trip-trap-trip-trap* all the goddamn day long." He waved the rifle as he talked, his arms big as footballs all the way around.

"You can't do this," the kid said, swallowing like he had a golf ball stuck in his throat.

Massey heard Zero in his head telling him what to do and he pointed the gun in the kid's face. "Can't do this? But I am. Bang." He told the kid to stand, told him to put his hands in the air. "All you have to give me," he said, "is your name, rank, and serial number. Geneva Convention." The kid blinked hard. "It's a joke, kid. Laugh." Then Massey marched him across the clearing into his shack, grabbed the clothesline on the way, tied the kid up using the knots a Charlie Company grunt had taught him over twenty years ago.

By the time the kid was all strapped in, the sun was starting to roll behind the stand of sugar pines on the other side of the marijuana patch. "Yell all you want," Massey told him. "Yell your head off. I got me one of them hoodoo juju spells working this place."

EVER SINCE GAIL LEFT, Massey stopped smoking bud. The stuff only spooked the shit out of him now.

"This isn't any life," she'd said to him and laughed the way she did at a bad joke. "I mean we're up here growing. But we're not."

She pointed her watercolor brush at the small clearing, at the leaves she'd been daubing with rainbow paints. She looked tired. Her arms and shoulders had become brown and leathery from years of working in the sun. Her hair, once the color of summer wheat, was streaked with coarse black strands now and some gray. The skin on her face had gone slack around the edges, like a little air was pumped under the surface, then sucked back out. "I love you," she'd said. "But not this. Not anymore. I want what's after this."

"Sweetheart," he'd said. He looked at her then, thought of the good days in Denny, Gail so young she used to show off the gymnastic floor routines she did in high school, cartwheeling, spinning between the rows of plants. "Sweetheart," he'd said and rubbed the down on the inside of her arm; some purple paint had dribbled a trail there. "You do anything long enough," he'd said, "that's what happens. Nothing grows forever. Not Jack's beanstalk even." He laughed like a horse snorting.

After saying it, he saw she was already gone. The blue in her eyes, once deep as the water in Tangle Blue Lake, now drained away to steel.

A week and a half later, when he was upstream tapping a new irrigation line into Lemonade Spring, the rest of her left. No note. Nothing. Just her ratty volume of fairy tales on the bed. Inside the front cover was the picture he'd snapped from one of those summers in Denny: Gail naked and standing in the shade of the monster fifteen-foot plant they'd managed to cultivate, she giving him a smile so big, it seemed he could make out every tooth in her mouth.

After she left, Massey saw something different in his little green meadow. The trees were the same. The madrones still peeled like wood shavings. The cones in the digger pines still cracked like knuckles in the heat of an August afternoon, dropped out of the sky like missiles every fall. And come April, Lemonade Spring still ran fat and fast from the melt, the same as it always did; two months later it would be spindle thin again, every speck in the granite river rock visible under the wrinkly, clear sheets of water.

The difference in the meadow was what he *didn't see*. The color was washed out of everything—like the way the photo of Gail under the plant was starting toward sepia, the way the leaves in the patch had to be recoated twice every growing season.

That was her idea, painting the leaves with watercolors. After Denny, the feds had turned ugly. The growers were forced to retreat into the woods and the government sent choppers over the national forest after them, the *whump whump whump* of the blades chasing them under the trees.

"It's the perfect camouflage," she'd said and was right. If a copter beat over toward Mad River, from the sky the plants would only look like harmless wildflowers in a mountain meadow: ceonothus, Indian paintbrush, alpine daisies, moon orchids, the like.

But after Gail left, he saw a sameness in all the different leaf pigments, a dullness that blunted, too, the green and brown serried hills, the red sumac in the draw beyond the sugar pines, the madrones, the morning sky, all of it.

And with all those edges filed down, what Massey saw was the gray trail that had led him finally to Lemonade Spring. It wended through Crescent City, Eureka, Mendocino, Fort Bragg—the summer after he was stateside again, when he and Zero sold Kansas ditch weed from a car trunk.

After that was Denny, a speck on the map up near Siskiyou County. Gail showed up one afternoon that first summer, worked the rows in her cutoffs and a short ribbed T.

"You were the kind of girl we talked about over there," Massey said to her one blue fall night, the buds already picked and hanging upside down and drying, moon coming up over the rise. He told her about when the boys couldn't slog any farther, when the rains in country came down like Jesus, the red highlands spurting water, his heart twisting in his chest retelling it. He told her about waiting out the weather, them trading memories of legs and hair and smiles, of honey and skin, the rain spattering their ponchos like enemy fire. "Wet dreams we called those girls," Massey said.

Gail stood, peeled off her shirt and shorts, standing there, skin white as the moon. Massey cried, had never seen anything so beautiful in his life. Gail held him and he cried, the cold night sweet as sugar on their skin, Gail jigging above him, her Buddha smile.

They grew into the life together. Until the feds came, they were sure they'd stay in Denny, live there happily ever after. But one summer a few USFS started scouting the woods. The next summer it turned into full-scale war, the DEA dropping out of the sky like Green Beret.

And after that it wasn't the same. Punji sticks. Bouncing Betties. Trip wires. It became every man for himself.

What Massey saw after Gail left was that his gray trail ended here in this grassy bowl near Lemonade Spring. He tried to leave at first but found he was rooted here. He could make it as far as the Spring, but beyond that, the woods closed around him, a jail of trunks.

The dogwood on the far side of the Spring became the edge of his world, where the trees met the water. Standing there one day shortly after Gail left, his packed duffel slung over his shoulder, he found that his feet couldn't move, were stuck fast to this ground. And he turned back, pulled the shade on the other side, the trees blocking out everything.

Massey planted himself in the garden, nurtured the red square of dirt, manicuring the lower leaves so air circulated and pests couldn't breed, spreading bear scat and dogwood compost over it, painting the upper canopy of leaves with watercolors three times during the season.

In the nights after Gail left, Massey sat on the planks outside the shack, the sweat cooling on him from the day's work, the moon coming up like a knobby face, reminding him of the story.

"I'll see you when the moon is full," he said, remembering what the archer said, how he climbed the sky once every month. But every month when the moon rose full over Lemonade Spring, Massey stayed, never found his way out of the trees and into the sky.

THE KID WAS QUIET for the first two days, didn't say much. Three times daily Massey undid the knots and marched him out to the hole for him to do his business.

Massey said, "Don't be bashful, kid. It's not good for you, keeping all that in."

He took to bringing the kid outside after the day's work was done. They sat on the planks, the kid strapped into the straightback chair, Massey in a lawn chair, watching evening come down, the first hints of the fall winds wrapping around September's hot edges.

The kid didn't look scared of him anymore, appeared to have gotten used to him clumping around the shack, big and gentle as a storybook bear. To Massey it seemed the kid was letting himself fall into the pull of his orbit up here, acting looser, friendlier, getting accustomed to the life.

"You got any people looking for you?" Massey said the fourth night.

"Probably not," the kid said.

Massey thought how young he looked, his jawline not yet dulled by years, hardly any stubble raised on his face. "Where your people expecting you to be?"

"Redding. At college," the kid said.

Massey sipped his beer. The bugs flew poky, stunned from the evening chill. He rubbed a finger along the broken line of his nose, snapped his hand out, caught a fly. "You sure nobody knows you came up here for your little hike?"

"It was fishing." The kid smiled at him. Massey tried to imagine what the kid's life would be like at college, but no image came to mind. "I'm sticking with fishing," the kid said.

"Good man," Massey said. He shook the hand with the fly in it like he was playing craps, opened it and watched the fly stumble back into the air. "You got something that works, stay with it."

The day was dying. The wind pushed down from Blue Point through Copper Hill, gathering speed along the South Fork, a ghost train carrying the smell of evergreens and cold water.

Sitting on the planks there, Massey felt the pull of the harvest. Every year it was the same. When the time came to prune the buds, he always felt as if a piece of him were being lopped off, too. In these lengthening fall nights, the air blew in from far away, the north, the gusts bringing in cold like an icy kiss.

He said, "It's a sad time of year." He undid one of the kid's arms, let him sip from the Etna Ale, the two of them taking turns sucking at the bottle as night dropped. He watched the kid when he wasn't looking, his profile in relief against the dark. It gave a flutter to see how much he looked like Zero, the picture Massey had in his head from when they lived above the gas station in Ruth those years ago.

Seeing the kid like that, he had questions swarming like bees in his head. This meadow was miles off Pack Trail, overland through ravines, granite drops, slash. Even if you wanted to find it, you couldn't. The kid must have known the way.

Stars leaked into the night sky. One fell in the northwest like a white thread pulling in the dark.

"Look at that," Massey said. The star fell behind the stand of trees now dark as ink blots. "It's a wonder they all don't fall," he said and lifted both hands, palms up.

The kid said, "It's not really a star. An asteroid or meteorite or cosmic debris maybe. The stuff burns up when it enters earth's atmosphere."

Massey took the empty from the boy's hand.

The kid pointed at the sky. "Astronomy." He swelled out his chest, talked about comets and quasars and black holes.

Massey chewed on the inside of his cheek, thinking about what the kid said, trying to understand it all, remembering the stories Gail had told about how the constellations got their names. He liked watching the kid talk, his free arm pointing, painting for Massey the picture he saw when he looked up.

"You make a wish?" Massey said. "Or is that just a load of cosmic debris, too?"

The kid laughed, his mouth pulling up on the right side into an off-kilter smile. "No," he said, "wishing's still cool."

Wind shook the plants in the garden. Massey laced the kid's arm to the chair again. Another star fell.

The kid said, "I did make one. A wish."

Massey nodded at him.

"I'm not telling it."

"It won't come true, right?" Massey said. He found himself rooting for the kid, pulling for whatever it was he'd wished for. For a moment, expectation prickled inside him like sweetness from a slice of sugar cake, then rose from his gut to his head, the thought it carried tripping him up: he hoped the kid was wishing to stay.

"That's birthdays," the kid said. A coyote barked from Bear Wallow. They listened to the night, the trees in the wind creaking like ship's rigging. "I don't think you'd like it," the kid said.

"Your wish?" Massey said. "Probably not."

THE QUESTION OF WHAT to do with the kid remained.

Massey was beginning to get attached to him, like a pet. Also he'd forgotten what it was like to be with people. He'd been alone so long, he'd become a stranger to his own voice. In the first few days he'd be telling the kid something and he'd stop in the middle, listen to his words rumble around the shack, have to remind himself to keep talking.

Massey felt bad about the ropes. He asked the kid if he wanted to be tied down flat during the nights in order to sleep better. "This is fine," the kid said, never complaining once. Massey still felt bad about it, considered what he could do to make things easier but never came up with anything.

One morning the second week, Massey had a dream with the kid in it. The dream started off with them both napping. Then he and the kid left the shack, walked over a rope bridge and up a hill. They were in Quang Tri muck, the rain, the kid in the trench next to him. "Don't shoot," the kid said, "until you see the red in their eyes." Massey laughed but what came out was birdsong. NVA crawled out from tunnels in the ground, smiling and bowing, putting flowers in the M-16s. "I have two sharp horns to poke you with," the kid said to the NVA.

When Massey woke, he could still smell the flowers, the sweetness drifting out of his head slowly. "I have two sharp horns to poke you with," he said and laughed.

The kid looked at him, trussed up there in the straightback, already awake. "What?" he said.

"Nothing," Massey said. "A dream."

The kid pulled at the ropes but there was no give, looked over at Massey. He smiled at the kid. "I bet you could do for some breakfast," he said. "I'm thinking of something a little different today." He got out the salt pork he'd been saving, sliced it into strips, and, when the pan was good and hot, placed them inside. The grease running out of the pork popped like firecrackers; Gail's apron on him was like a too-small dress.

When the pork was cooked, Massey fried up peppers, then mixed in eggs. The shack filled with the heavy smell of grease and salt. It reminded him of the old days when he'd cooked for Gail, making the recipes she'd liked, names he'd never heard of but were delicious just the same.

"It isn't the Waldorf," he said to the kid, giving him a plate. "Hope you like it." He cut up the pork for him, untied one arm.

The two of them ate the special breakfast in silence. Massey watched the sun come up over the trees, these days lower and lower every morning, its arc now a sidearm throw.

He could harvest the buds anytime. He liked to wait on clipping them. He'd douse the plants once more and stopper up the PVC pipes for the season. Then for a few days he'd let the sun bake them. Zero said this pushed the THC from the stems into the buds. They turned purply as they dried out and became flecked with crystals like Frosted Flakes.

Today he'd drive the line deeper into Lemonade Spring. The water was running with hardly any force now. In the mornings and nights he could feel the wetness on the northerlies, but the rains wouldn't start for weeks.

The kid was looking out the Plexi window at the patch, the

food scoured off his tin plate. "Weird shit," he said, pointing at the colored leaves. "Smells fucking kickass."

"Indica sativa hybrid," Massey said and explained how they'd taken indica, a sleepy high, and combined it with sativa, which was more uppity. "The yield's better with indica," he said. "Sativas are sparse. The trick of it is getting the right mix of yield and kick." He thought of Zero, who called it dialing in the variables, always developing new cuttings under his indoor lights in Mad River.

"Who's this *we?*" the kid said.

Massey watched him, wondering how much he knew about the operation, wanted to say, "Stop shitting me," but didn't. It *might* just be coincidence. "Never you mind," he said to the kid. He went over to the straightback and tied his arm down with the Charlie boy knots.

"You know what we should do?" the kid said. "We should roll ourselves a fatty. Smoke it." He smiled at Massey as if the two of them were in on a secret.

Then the kid talked about college, the shit they smoked there. Massey had a hard time following all of it. The kid and his friends had built a four-foot bong out of PVC piping. "Just like the stuff I saw in your garden," he said. "It's got this carburetor, right? You can shotgun-smoke until your head explodes." He told Massey about how he and his friends got stoned, then surfed some kind of net on the computer. Massey nodded, liked hearing the kid talk, the words coming out faster than the April current, but he didn't understand it, couldn't imagine it. He could only see as far as the edge of Lemonade Spring. Beyond that it was as if there was a screen, what the kid said lost in shadows.

The kid told another thing they would do, a game called assassin. A secret list was drawn up and everybody in the game had a secret killing they had to carry out. With each successful hit, the assassin took over the victim's assigned killing, the list eventually working its way down to two, then to one assassin, the winner.

"Killed?" Massey said.

"We use tennis balls," the kid said. "Symbolic. You never know when it's coming."

The kid grew quiet. Massey thought he must have been thinking about college, maybe a girl he had there or the fun they had playing assassin and surfing the nets. Massey decided there was something in his eyes that wasn't like Zero but couldn't figure what it was.

When he saw the kid's face squeeze into a sorry wince, he got up and collected the plates and the frying pan, busying himself, trying to ignore the sharp feeling he had in his chest from watching the kid go sulky. He thought the kid might cry.

"You play basketball at that school of yours?" he asked, trying to draw him out.

"No," the boy said.

Massey finished cleaning up. For days he'd ignored the ropes that strapped the kid in, not the tying-him-up part but what the ropes meant.

He found he could talk to the kid, tell him things that had been gathering like a cloud inside him, about living off the grid for so long, and in those times the ropes melted away and it was Massey who was held fast there, not the kid.

He looked over his shoulder at him as he cleaned, the kid pulling at the ropes again.

"You can't keep me here," the kid said. "I know what you growers do, okay? If you're going to kill me, kill me. You can't keep me here."

Massey tried to find words to soothe the kid, but his mouth was rusted machinery. He fiddled with the gas jet on the Coleman stove. He wanted to tell the kid what a single day of sunlight looked like in the meadow after a week of winter rain, how swamped he'd get from all the smells of spring, how early-summer days were as perfectly formed as a bubble, about the sweet loss of fall. He started to tell him but his words stopped, couldn't go any further.

And he went outside with a heaviness that stayed with him all day as he watered the patch for the last time of the season.

When he peeked in the Plexi window, he saw the kid was still droopy, a waterlogged tree. It was a warm September harvest day, a picture of Indian summer, but Massey never felt it.

He ran the flexible hose deeper in Lemonade Spring that afternoon, barely enough water in the current now to suck at the rocks. And hiking back to the cabin, the moon coming up, nearly full, he saw the dark of the woods close around him, a locked door.

THE KID DIDN'T TALK all that night and the next day, refused the food Massey cooked up for him. Massey tried to think of different ways to rig the knots so he'd have more freedom, but no better system came to mind.

He talked to the kid anyway. "It's aiming to be a hot one," he said in the morning. "That's good. The plants like that." The sun was coming up big over the firs, the smell from the garden thicker than skunk. "I'll be back," he said to the kid. "Don't you go anywhere," he said and gave a gentle laugh.

Working the plot, Massey couldn't shake the sad picture of the kid. The soil without its daily watering was going toward loamy again. He counted the buds on every plant. It would be a good year. He thought how happy Zero would be.

In the heat of the day—the thermometer on the grape stake read ninety-two degrees—the kid and Zero merged in Massey's head and he went back years to the apartment over the gas station in Ruth, after the summer of selling ditch weed, after he was state-side again. Their money was running toward empty. Spring was hitting then, exploding crayons outside the window, the Trinities leafing out. The sky was so clear it went on forever, just sky and color and shrinking winter snowcaps.

Zero was on the bed in the corner, the angles of his face as sharp as right turns. "They might as well have sent you back in a box," he'd said. "The way you are."

Massey was practicing the knots the Charlie boy grunt had shown him.

Zero looked at him from across the room. "Options," he'd said. "You got any?" He stood up and paced across the chipped linoleum floor, the smell of lube and oil everywhere. "You got any?"

Massey had thought the ditch weed was just a lark. But the world he'd come home to seemed out of register with the one he'd left. There'd been men on the moon; he couldn't believe that. He'd look up at it after he returned, tried to imagine men up there in the geometry of the stars, the wonder.

"Any plans?" Zero said.

Massey didn't say. He thought about it, tested the Charlie boy knots he was tying. But he couldn't think clearly, his thoughts and the knots around him like a mouth.

"AWOL," Zero said. "Permanently," he said, tapping his head, what Massey'd heard before except with different words. "Don't worry. I got a plan." Zero looked just like a wizard, an attitude that was all cock and walk.

In the garden now Massey heard Zero's words again. "Don't worry, kid," he said to himself. "I'll think of something."

THE NEXT NIGHT WAS clear and cold after another hot after-noon. It seemed to Massey as he worked the patch that the sun was trying to climb back up to the middle of the sky but couldn't, was too tired after all the long days of summer.

Fall was settling in the mountains; he felt it, the pull of earth rhythms. The crops were nearly in. Tomorrow he'd prune the buds off the plants. After that he'd wait for Zero to make one last trip up to Lemonade Spring to carry out the harvest, Zero dragging his way into the meadow with his pack and travois, loaded to the teeth with guns and ammo like a cartoon bandito, humping in the supplies Massey would need to last him until spring.

Tonight, inside him, what Massey felt was warmth, like fire, not the usual loss he had for summer passing into fall. He'd come to a decision about the kid. He was thinning back the leaves to expose the buds when it hit him. He'd offer him a cut in the oper-ation. Thinking more about it, he figured Zero knew all along, what with the kid looking like his young double; it was one of Zero's tests, he decided, but didn't understand, not exactly, what that test was. What he did know was if the kid stayed on, they could clear more land, increase the yield. It was something to talk about with Zero.

When Massey entered the shack in early evening, he was jaunty from all the new plans, wore the mood like it was a new hat. "Honey," he said, "I'm home." The kid didn't bother looking up, his eyes staring at the rough floor, lashes a half-inch long, easy.

Massey put a bud the size of a small pinecone in front of him. The kid smiled for the first time in days.

"The fruit of my labors," Massey said. He found papers in the rickety box he'd nailed together into a chest, rolled a joint that looked like a white zeppelin, untied the kid's arm, lit the joint.

He'd forgotten the sweet taste. Their smoke poured into the room, like wind, Massey thought, a gray, indigo wind. The kid sucked on the joint like it was a teat. His sad eyes went to happy and red, the rims closing from the smoke and the high that was coming on. "Damn," he said. "Damn. Damn."

Massey accepted the joint from him, said, "What's your name?"

"Wyatt."

They both laughed at that, the kid giggling like a girl. "Gunslinger name," Massey said and laughed more, the picture in his head of when he first spied the kid in the garden, Massey poking the sawed-off muzzle in his back. "Some gunslinger," he said.

They talked about how good the dope was. The kid praised Massey to the skies. "You're an artist. Unbelievable."

Massey bowed from the waist in the chair he was sitting in. He'd forgotten the feeling of how everything inside expanded. He thought his head was growing, bald spot getting bigger on his crown, and he ran his hand through his hair; his head was the size of a pumpkin.

"That ain't coming back, bro," the kid said and exploded in coughs and smoke and barking sniggers. He put his hand up for a high five and Massey thought he was waving and waved back and tears came out of the kid's eyes, he was laughing so hard. The kid tried to get serious, as if putting on a mask, and he cracked up all over again. "This stuff kills," he said.

They smoked another joint. Time slowed. Massey thought if he could catch the moment and put it in a bottle, fall would never come, he could live forever right now. He looked out the window, saw night, the air not black but blue and navy, the sky over the sugar pines still holding the amber of sunlight, a memory. He thought about telling the kid of his plans, felt his stomach floating.

The kid was looking at him now, a question swimming in watery eyes. "Vietnam," he said, "must have been freaky shit or something."

"It was something," Massey said. "Definitely something." He told him about the green tracers sailing overhead like fireflies on steroids, the F-105s dropping ordnance. "Me and a few of the boys liked to watch them from this hill," he said. "They'd take off, fly north." He held his hand flat and showed the kid, told him about lighting up the Thai dope they called pixie stick, watching the hills bang and scorch in the distance.

"Fuck," the kid said.

"Those knots," Massey said, pointing with the joint at the kid. "Those knots I learned over there. Some Charlie boy grunt showed me outside Cam Lo. See him every day in my head like it's today. We're humping the hillside when we come across his company. 'I got me one more month,' Charlie boy says. Had blond hair that was white. Missing front tooth. Two days later we hear his whole outfit was greased." Massey drew hard on the joint. "Those knots," he said, blowing smoke. "NVA knots. The more you push, the tighter it gets. Expect you know that already."

"Jesus," the kid said. He looked like a child who'd been told a scary bedtime story. His head bobbed, taking it all in.

"You seen the shit I seen," Massey said, "you know pigs fly."

They smoked the joint not saying anything, their pulls sounding like the lamp drawing on its propane canister behind Massey.

The kid's serious face suddenly broke like ice, laughter punching through again. "The sixties, man," he said, his voice loopy and elastic.

Massey smiled at him, thought about telling him his plan now, how he and the kid could make a life of it up here, but the kid was having such a good time he didn't want to interrupt.

"You got a favorite Dead song?" the kid said.

"I do," Massey said. "The short one." And their joy in the little shack sounded like animal noises.

Massey rolled another joint, happy to see the kid's spirits climb like this. He saw again something in the kid's eyes that wasn't Zero. "It's a good life up here," Massey said, lighting the joint. "Make-believe almost."

He started telling the kid what it was like, had it in mind to slowly steer to the subject of his staying. "It's real magic," he said and described the earth pull he always felt rooting him to this ground. He told of the weather that brought the black bears down from the hills, them rolling down the slope like big cannonballs sometimes, about the bats that came out of the trees spring nights, a crazy flying ballet.

His words dragged him away from the conversation he had in mind; he saw his plan growing distant in his head, sliding through his hands like rope. "This place has a real hold on me," he said. "Strong," he said, then softer, "strong." His eyes went wet. "I can't break away," he said.

The tears in his eyes were a prism. He waved his hand, shooed the thoughts lining up in his mind, saw a wake of colored lines, trails following his hand—lollipop reds, bottle blues, celery greens.

He saw the kid through the teary film, the kid biting his lip, eyelashes that were brushes, his beard in heavier now but still soft. He tried to tell the kid of his plan but he was underwater, crying.

The dope hit like a bomb in his head, the room going rubbery. Massey was so tired. He shut his eyes, listened to the rushing in his head, drifted to a place of static and humming.

HE DIDN'T KNOW HOW long he was out. When he opened his eyes he saw the kid pointing the gun in his face. "Wyatt," he said, his voice like dropping dew.

"Halt," the kid said. "Who goes there?"

"Wyatt. You and me. This place."

The kid jabbed the muzzle in Massey's chest, said louder, "Who goes there?"

Then Massey saw it—the kid's eyes, brown like a deer's, not Zero's spruce green. Then he saw the rest. The bones in the kid's face shifted; he didn't look like Zero anymore, just a twenty-year-old kid who'd hiked up here because he'd heard he could rip off the growers in these hills. And everything went slack inside Massey, became unbound.

He shrunk down in his seat, tried to pull into himself, disappear. "Wyatt," he said. "Come on. Cool. Be cool," he said. "You're a Popsicle." He knew what was coming next like he'd been waiting all his life for it, thought of that poor son of a bitch VC, just the stem of his neck left and pulp where the head had been.

He wanted to pray but couldn't think of one, felt the release anyway. He blinked hard and finally saw beyond the trees on the other side of Lemonade Spring, felt the spell broken and could see all the way to a place that was blue and gauzy and he knew what this place was and he wasn't scared anymore.

"Who goes there?" the kid said.

"It's only me," Massey said.

WHEN MASSEY CAME TO, he remembered it was only the rock salt in the gun. The shack was pitch. The blast must have shattered the propane lantern. He smelled the smoke from the blast in the room, tasted the powder on his face, and his blood, salty, warm, running like lava from ear to ear.

There was a lightness. He tried to stand but couldn't; the kid had tied him to the chair. It wasn't the Charlie boy knots, and after some work he slipped out of it. He felt light and wasn't sure in the black room if his feet were on the ground.

It wasn't right, the room. Massey couldn't find the door. He searched the walls with his hands, little splinters from the rough wood sticking his fingers like needles. He found the metal hinges, kicked the door open.

Outside fall had come, entered the meadow completely, the sky a midnight blue, everything around him different shades of gray and cotton, like a negative.

Massey walked out into the patch. The buds had been clipped off. The moonlight shone and he could see what little was left of the plants—stems and broken leaves and roots.

He felt it again, the lightness. The moon shone so bright, it seemed on fire. He looked up: a full harvest moon that ate up the sky, bigger than any he'd ever seen before.

And it made sense to Massey then that a cow could jump over it. It was made of cheese and butter; it cut a milk path through the woods and he drank it in. Massey followed the path and the woods opened up for him and he walked farther than he had in years, beyond Lemonade Spring, which was barely gurgling now, walked into the middle of the purple forest.

And he kept following the moon.

A Dream She Had

THESE WOODS ARE FULL of strange music. Maybe that's why Carmella doesn't realize it's a bear that's crashed into their lives. But most likely it's because she doesn't want to hear what's out there.

What she hears sounds like the roll of timpani in the third movement of Verdi's *Requiem.* Or perhaps a far-off storm. But not the wildness. It's a clear day, only a ghosted splinter of moon hanging in an eggshell sky.

It's nothing, Carmella tells herself, remembering the thousands of sounds she used to hear in the city, traffic and dogs and neighbors, all the hum and noise that ran through her as silently as her own blood. It's only the country, she thinks, and starts the motor, pumping water into the thousand-gallon tank that supplies their cabin. And the sound of that tears a hole in the afternoon.

When the tank is full, water spitting out from the pipe at the top, Carmella switches off the engine. All she hears is the wash of China Creek coming through the glade of sugar pines and oaks, cedars and Douglas firs; wind like a distant locomotive chug-

chugging up the small runnel on the other side of the creek; screeches and hoots and woodnotes.

Then she hears it again, follows it back, walking beyond the pump house, through the stand of slash, up the small berm, and finally to the mouth of the old well. The tin lid isn't covering the opening anymore and the sound, now like big kettles knocking together, is coming from inside. Looking over the rim, she sees the lid hung up on a thin ledge fifteen feet down, and below that, five feet lower in total darkness, is something big and black and moving.

Carmella runs for the phone. Harry isn't in the office. They're wiring their corner of the county for service, she's told; he could be anywhere.

She has some question about whom to call next. Back in San Francisco the Yellow Pages were the stuff of circus-strongman-ripping legend—two fat volumes to cover the whole alphabet, the answer always somewhere inside. But up here, Salyer, the entire Trinity County phone book, yellow and white pages combined, is so thin, sixty pages at most, Carmella could easily tear it in half herself.

Ultimately she decides on fish and game. "There's something in our well," she says to the man who answers, realizing at once how silly this sounds. "I don't mean water, of course. An animal. A deer, I think. I'm not sure. I couldn't look."

All she hears on the other end is the dispatcher radio crackling like fire. People up here always pause before they talk, as if constantly having to catch their breath. "How about us starting at the beginning?" he says. "Why don't you tell me who you are first, your name."

Carmella flaps her hand, tells him. About their little cabin that sits like a tilty hat above the copse of secondary growth. About how far they've come from the city to get where they are—north of the

Central Valley, west across the shoulders of the Trinities, north and west to the ridge in Salyer that snugs up close to the Humboldt County line. "My husband Harry inherited the place from some uncle," she says. "Calvin, I think it was. Maybe Chester. It was one of those kind of names."

"Okay," he says. "Now tell me about the well."

She looks out the window toward the berm. "The well? I don't know what I can tell you. It's not in use anymore."

"Any water in it?"

Carmella shakes her head. "I never thought of that. Can deer swim?" she says. The picture of deer treading water suddenly seems entirely improbable. "I can check," she says. "About the water."

Again the pause. "No," he answers finally. "Why don't you sit tight until we get there. It doesn't sound like you're in any danger. Don't worry, I'm sending my men right away to your place."

His voice is smooth, thick as velour. Carmella can see why he has this job, answering the phones. "What a lifesaver," she says. "You are—?"

"Oren," he says. "One of those names."

THE SUN IS BARELY making it to the top of the giant pon-derosa these days. When the wind comes down off Sawtooth now it's cold, from somewhere else, from out of the north. Harry says he remembers the snows from when he was a kid. Bigger than the cabin, he says.

But the season isn't what Carmella thinks about walking down the quarter-mile dirt drive to unlock the gate for fish and game. She knows all too well where the animal down there has come from. It's the same place everything else has: her curse.

Six months ago, in March, when they were still living in San Francisco, God tried to punish Carmella but missed. It can happen. The rainy season was only starting to lift its foggy skirt.

On that evening in particular, in the witchy hours of night, the sky was wearing an extra layer of muslin. Carmella remembers. She got up to go to the bathroom, had the taste of Edward DeLuca, the Laurel Heights Ensemble's violinist, still in her mouth from that afternoon. After she returned to bed and back to sleep in the gray night was when it happened. Two feet to the right and it would have been Carmella, the rightful target, and not Harry.

On the very same bed thirteen hours earlier Edward had plucked her as delicately as he did his antique Guarneri. Those fingers: watching them move up and down the neck of his violin in rehearsals reminded her of the finches at the feeder outside her living room window, a fluttering of wings. His other hand held the bow so gently it almost wasn't holding it at all, his long, tapering, nearly feminine fingers curling into a cave around the bow, each pink nail having the even symmetry of a sidewalk square.

His fingers were as far as it went. It wasn't love, this thing with Edward. Even lying in his arms she knew Harry was love, knew he was true and giving, sweet and for keeps. Any man could buy flowers like the spray of dahlias and baby tears Edward had brought her. But Harry, he was the kind of man who not only brought flowers but built window boxes to plant them in.

That afternoon had nothing to do with Harry and everything with her. It was about being married for six years and seeing their coffee mugs in the same place in the kitchen sink every weekday morning, about hearing the magic Edward's fingers could produce and wanting, just this once, to follow.

She had dreamed those hours together would be the way Mozart skipped off Edward's bow, perfect as math, magical, a precise passion that would run to the very center of her, fill her up. In her head it was a witty, metropolitan picture she'd painted, a trifling romance that, like the neighborhood's number 3 Jackson bus, would only go so far but no farther.

What she found afterward was only a fat violinist sleeping like a mutt, tip of his tongue sticking out of his teeth. And across the bedroom in the mirror Carmella saw herself—long, heather hair direct from the Italian Alps, gently arching aquiline nose, bosom that at thirty-five was still glorious, still as full and rich and round as a whole note. And at that moment she knew it was that, her reflection, a curse of vanity, that had actually cast the spell, not the beauty Edward's fingers could produce.

It was just the once with Edward but that was enough. What Carmella woke to the next day was an ugly mass of pulp and skin on Harry's pillow. "My God, Harry," she said. "Your head's inflated like a basketball." And it was. Gone were the cheekbones sheer as steeples, jaw square as the state lines of Wyoming, smile sweeter than manna. "Baby, what on earth has happened?" she said but already knew the answer to the question.

"I don't know, Carly," Harry said, testing himself gently with fingertips, then getting up to look at himself in the mirror. "Jesus, I look like the nephew of the Elephant Man."

It got worse. "Do you have any pets?" the doctor asked. His office smelled exactly like the kind of soap Carmella used to wash her face with when she was a teenager.

"Fish," she said. "We have neon tetras. Two catfish that clean the algae from the tank. Some of those, I don't know what they're called. Angel fish, I think."

"No dogs or cats?"

"No," she said.

"I don't like saying this," he said, "but you're going to have to get rid of the fish."

"But they're underwater."

Harry laughed, face fleshy, sallow as an onion, eyes goggly, the sound of it like clucking, not laughter. It was a painful thing for her to watch. "Carly, honey, where else would fish be?" he said.

"I mean we don't come in contact with them," she said, looking to him, then the doctor.

"You don't need to." The doctor cleaned his glasses, put them back on, frowned, breathed on them, cleaned them again. "The virus can become airborne from the surface of the water, if that's what indeed is causing Harry's acute dermatitis. In any case, the fish go." In the reflection in his lenses, her face was as misshapen as Harry's.

"So what do we do about Harry?" Carmella asked.

"We'll put him on a regimen of medication. There will be a lot of pills and injections at first. Until we know what works, what takes."

Carmella said, "What about side effects? What about babies?" She pictured flushing them down the toilet, too.

"Are you planning on a family?" He ran his thumb down Harry's chart, sneaked a glance at the wall clock.

"No, we aren't. Not yet."

"Well, there might be a problem with the medication," he said and mentioned a catalog of words as if ticking off a shopping list: depressed sperm count and lack of motility, temporary sterility, potential for impotency. "The first year it's a crapshoot," he said. "After that the situation usually stabilizes. Then the medication can be reduced to a maintenance level and your chances should increase back to near normal."

"Is that one of your new medical terms," Carmella said, "crapshoot?" Harry tapped her hand, rubbed her forearm. The doctor didn't say anything.

She knew better about the fish but kept the dark truth to herself, and later that night, hoping on the skinny possibility that the doctor was correct, she scooped them up in a plastic bag and placed them in the freezer, on top of the frozen orange juice. This was a far more humane way of disposing of them, she was told, freezing them. An hour later their color was practically gone, the fish hard as stones, a pocketful of cloudy, washed-out agates and jades.

Harry didn't get better. Carmella added the fish to the darkness steeping inside her. His head became puffed as a dinner roll. "Just pop me in the oven," he said, "and I'll be ready to eat in no time." But Carmella couldn't laugh, had taken to wearing black as if mourning.

At the home where Carmella played her flute for the terminally ill, Eunice Schwartz noticed the black. "Did you lose someone, dear?" she asked.

Thinking of the fish, of Harry, her eyes flitting like sixteenth notes, Carmella couldn't talk at first. "Oh yes," she said eventually. "It was . . . A whole school was wiped out."

The old woman huffed, went rheumy around the eyes, passed her hand over the clumps of hair that hadn't yet been knocked out by chemo. "Good Lord. Were they little?"

"Very," Carmella said, spreading her thumb and index finger an inch to show her.

"You'll be in my prayers."

"Thank you."

And when Eunice reached over, ran her chapped hand along Carmella's face, Carmella felt the truth in her growing crazy, deadly, ugly like a tumor, felt it climbing right out of her. "I'm sorry, Eunice, I have to go now," she said and left the room, ran down the hall to the bathroom, dropped her flute on the floor of the stall, threw up. But it didn't eliminate the blackness spreading inside her.

That evening as Carmella marinated salmon for dinner she didn't notice her blue-sapphire world outside the kitchen window: the bay and the sky, Angel Island winking in the surface haze, the finger of Point Reyes reaching out into the Pacific way off in the distance, a foghorn near the Marin footing of the Golden Gate Bridge sounding, a lonely tuba.

Inside the room was dark as ink. She still reeled from how dreadful she'd been with Eunice. With the wet, pliant salmon in her hands, suddenly everything was too much for Carmella and she opened the freezer, removed the foil-wrapped packets of halibut and swordfish and mahi-mahi, and tried to flush the whole mess down the toilet but they wouldn't go, just circled the bowl.

THE ANIMAL IN THE well isn't the first thing that's fallen into Carmella's life today. That morning there had been something else. Harry had already left for work and the sun was only starting to define the ragged edge of treetops behind the cabin. It was cold these mornings; the madrone in the woodstove that Harry relit before leaving was just then taking. In the bathroom Carmella shifted from one foot to the other on the cold linoleum. She read the box. Pink was for positive. Hers was the color of healthy flesh.

She couldn't think of it then, seven hours ago, can't now. After all she's done — Harry, the fish, Eunice, having to move up here to Salyer — the thought of her being a mother, that something could still be unspotted from the thing inside her that's grown like a pitchy fungus, seems as improbable as deer swimming.

Now the three men from fish and game shine a light down the well. The little one with the fat face, eyes green as the trees up on Hyampom, enough hair for only a top-knot, whistles, hikes up trousers, turns back to Carmella. Brady his name is. "I've got a little surprise for you," he says.

She nods.

"That's not a deer. It's a bear."

The one next to Oren, Fess, spits some juice, cheeks working like an agitator on an old washing machine, brown bushy sideburns rising, falling. He turns back to look down the well, says, "Holy shit. It's a real monster. Look at that head. Biggest one I've ever seen. Must be a four-hundred-pounder, a male I'd say."

Oren says, "He must have ridden that tin lid down like it was a sled or something." He smiles at Carmella, his dark eyes kind and wise. "It's okay to look," he says to her. "That bear's not going anywhere."

And she does. The bear is standing in three feet of water looking up, breathing heavy, head as wide as the top of a garbage can, eyes that seem to hold a world of sorrow, fur blacker than coal. When it sighs, Carmella almost mistakes it for human. "He looks so beautiful," she says.

"It's a dump bear probably," Brady says. "Most probably tastes exactly like what it's been eating. Garbage."

Fess rubs the string of chewing dottle off his lips. "At this angle we couldn't even manage a heart shot."

"What's that?" Carmella asks. "A heart shot."

He taps just above the pocket on her denim shirt, the feel of it going right through her. Over in their truck she sees their rifle on the mount and something inside her sinks. She knows now how this will end.

"Don't worry," Oren says. "It's not going to come to that. We couldn't possibly kill something this grand. Do you have a ladder?" he says.

Carmella leads Brady past the cabin to the generator shack, the two of them returning with the ladder. The men extend it on the ground next to the well, locking the stops in place, then feed the ladder down inside. It hits the bear on the shoulder, bounces against the side, makes a dull, bass tuning-fork sound and he grumbles, tries to swat at it. Eventually he seems to understand what the ladder's for, rests back on the corrugated well wall, and the men inch the ladder down to the bottom.

Oren pulls on the rungs sticking out the top, trying to lessen the angle. "If this works," he says, "be prepared to run." Then to Carmella, "You might want to go for the house now."

But it's already clear there's too much bear at the bottom, the ladder leaning only a few clicks south of ninety degrees. Inside the well the bear rests an arm on a lower rung.

"That's not going to work," Brady says. "What next?"

Carmella says, "I bet you'd like some coffee," and the three of them agree and she heads back to the cabin. Mid-afternoon is coming on; the sun is poking up over the enormous Douglas fir down by the creek like the top of an orange-yellow big toe.

Walking back to the cabin, she hears a growl from the well, one of the men saying something she can't hear, Fess laughing. The wind picks up, knocking down pink and red dogwood leaves.

On the kitchen counter the coffee machine breathes hard, steam coming out the drip, the last of the water already in the filter. Carmella tries to imagine what's inside her, listens, feels nothing. She watches the men out the window. They lean against a tree talking, Brady smoking.

CARMELLA IS PLAYING THE flute when Harry drives up, Handel's Sonata in A Minor. When she comes outside he's already talking to the men. He smiles at her, turns away from them, walks over to her.

"You're home early," she says.

Harry is better, the lines of his face already redrawn to the easy handsomeness that can still cross Carmella's wires. It was sick building syndrome, what he had in the city. "Microbes," he said when they finally found out in April.

"Microbes?" she asked.

"Little microscopic organisms in the building at work." Harry exploded with coughs as he explained it. "They don't know if it's the air-circulation system, the heating, the air conditioning, what have you. It could be any number of things—agents, they call them."

"Cooties, you mean," she said, pushing her hair behind her ears.

The next week Harry told her about his idea of moving up to Salyer to flee the microbes. Inside her she felt the real truth of the situation, her curse, eating away at her stomach like a solvent. But all she said was "How's leaving the city going to cure anything? Cooties are everywhere. It's an established fact of nature."

But they drove so far from the city they eventually outran the radio. Dizzy Gillespie's "Tin Tin Deo" called out from the speakers like an old friend, Carmella transposing the notes in her head, practicing the fingering of the jabby horn lines on her leg.

Three hours on I-5 and Harry's face was still cranberry, his breath coming in wheezes, rattles, not unlike the wonky vacuum cleaner they sold at the moving sale. The July day was hot enough to bake pottery, the freeway running straight as a gun shot, the spine of the Central Valley exactly how she pictured hell, except with grass.

At Redding, Carmella and Harry left the freeway. There were smaller blue routes and country western. Later, surface roads and farm reports. Eventually the only road to Salyer and no radio at all.

With Brady smoking by the well opening, Fess and Oren talking off by the truck, Harry puts his arm around her shoulders.

He smells the way he always does now: of trees and wind and earth. "You think I'd miss this?" he says. "I have to admit when I got the field call, I was afraid you might have been picking mushrooms or something. It's a bear, you know, not a deer."

"I know," she says.

He squeezes her arm. "It's perfect. Absolutely perfect," he says and turns, walking back to the men. "Hey, fellas, I have an idea." Harry is the kind of man who still uses the word *fellas*. Seeing him describing what he's thinking, arms moving up and down, touching Fess's shoulder, Oren studying him intently, little Brady nodding as if his head was spring-loaded—seeing all this, Carmella knows why the phone company in Cedar Flat offered him a job the first day he walked into the office.

"That could work," Oren says. Harry leads Brady to the phone and the two other men discuss the logistics of his plan. In half an hour a truck from P&H Towing drives up and fifteen minutes later the vet.

"All right," Harry says and waves his arms, directing the driver back toward the mouth of the well. "It has to be a slipknot," he tells Oren after the truck's in place and starts rigging it. When he's done Oren drops it down the well, the sling falling over the bear's head.

"The knot isn't slipping," Fess says.

"Pull harder," Harry says. When the knot finally does release, the sling isn't pulling tight enough around the bear. "Okay," Harry says. "That's not going to work. Let's pull it off. I'll redo it."

The string comes back up the well, Harry reloops the rope, and this time when Oren throws it back down the well, it catches around the bear's head and front leg.

"You see that?" Brady says. "That bear didn't even try to avoid it. Like it knows what's going on." The bear bites at the rope a little, looks back up the shaft at the men and Carmella.

"Pull," Harry says. The ropes break away, the sling pulls tight. Next the vet climbs down the ladder, ten-foot jab pole with tranquilizer tip in his hand, hits the bear twice with the syringe, the bear complaining.

They stand around for fifteen minutes waiting for the tranquilizer to take. "Honey, why don't you go inside," Harry says. When she sees them from the front window of the cabin, the men look blotty, the edges of them getting lost in the shadow and dark of early evening.

The truck starts up, the cable starts spooling in. When the bear lifts up out of the top the driver guns the engine, the truck popping forward, and the bear flies three feet from the well, landing, stepping out of the sling, standing up, looking at the crowd of men. They scatter like duckpins. The bear lumbers off.

IT'S SEVEN FORTY-FIVE that same night and from the window of the cabin Carmella can see none of the trees, only her reflection on the glass.

"That was something," Harry says. He's elated. "What a perfect ending." Right after the bear left, the men crowded around him, slapped him on the back. Brady even hugged him. Harry came back in for the bottle of tequila and shot glasses. "You want one?" he'd said to Carmella. "You want to come outside with us?"

"It's a guy thing, I'm sure," Carmella had said. "I'm happy to watch all you standing around and scratching yourselves from here."

Now just the two of them there, Harry goes over to the refrigerator. "Do you smell propane?" he says.

Carmella sniffs, recognizes the inky Magic Marker smell. "Now that you mention it, I do."

He opens the bottom of the rickety old Servel, pulls out the metal tube, relights the pilot, blows into the tube to create the sideways draft. The Freon heating element is cold and it takes a while. He blows for ten minutes. Finally the flame is coherent, a thumb of blue that points horizontally.

When Carmella sees him, red as a bing cherry from blowing, she's stopped short. "I don't deserve you," she says. "You are too good." And she picks up her flute, still on the table from this afternoon, and walks outside.

Once away from the cabin, she finds that it's not so dark, the stars leaking tiny, spurry light in the navy bowl of the night sky. Off behind her the generator gargles gently in its shack. Carmella takes the little winding path to China Creek, sits on the redwood bench under the giant, old-growth Douglas fir, tries Handel's Sonata in A Minor again.

After they moved to Salyer, Harry cemented the bench into the ground, the posthole digger sparking whenever it struck rock, he cursing "Fucking bench, fucking bench" every kiss of metal on stone. Two days after, the cement set like granite, he said, "Let's go down to the fucking bench." Flat on her back on top of it, her hands made a beard of knuckles and nails on his cheeks. Harry pumped away, his face moving above her from extreme close-up to mid-range. The branches waved like palsied arms. A gibbous moon hung in the early night like a blasted plate of china.

Now the notes of the sonata become shapes she can't draw with her flute, the notes running away from her. Carmella gets up, walks along the bank. She trips over the flexible tubing that leads from the creek to the pump house, follows the path of the tubing, then turns toward the berm.

The ladder is still in the well. With flute wedged under her arm, she climbs down and rests her feet on a rung above the water, her back leaning on the corrugated sides that are too dark to bounce a reflection back, her body curved like a clef. The nutty smell of bear scat hovers over the water, thick and almost sweet.

She plays her flute. It is not the sonata this time but something else, what Carmella hears inside her—the strange music that is there. The notes pour out, climbing all the way up to Ursa in the sky.

From above a voice: "That's beautiful," Harry says. "What is it?"

"It's nothing. I mean I'm making it up as I go."

"It's beautiful," he says. Then, "I knew about it, Carmella. It doesn't matter."

She says nothing, looks up at the featureless head, the sky behind it.

"Keep playing," he says. "I'll be here when you're ready to come up."

When he retreats from the opening of the well, she puts the flute to her mouth again. Down here, the notes spinning up the shaft from the black bottom, the city seems only like a dream she had. This is real: the bear funk in the water; Harry up there waiting, probably straightening the slat of siding that's come loose from the back of the pump house; the wind blowing off Sawtooth cold and clear; living up here in Salyer; this pinkish thing that came into her life this morning.

It is not sweet harmony coming from her flute but it is music, a heart shot. "Harry," she calls up to him.

His head reappears. "Yes, Carly?"

Climbing up the ladder, she says, "Can I tell you something you don't know?" And what she tells him as she steps out of the well, what she finally tells him is what is inside her, and that is the most beautiful music she's ever heard.

Ice the Color of Sky

It was a long way to go to put Tom Wesley's body in the ground. When Gavin left Coldfoot in the morning, the dogs were still hungry for the run, the snow, baying like crazy in the kennels back of the house.

His mushing was all but over, spring now poking into the day's fat middle, white giving way to mud, the dogs' winter coats going soon to mange.

He caught a flight out of the bush after he finally got the word, left the team in Smitty's care. Eight days it was that his older brother, Tom Wesley, had been dead.

Gavin was up the Sag River the whole of the time, he and the dogs. It was the pull. That's what had brought him to that emptiness of wavy hills, snow and ice, the deep tug he'd felt all winter in the long days of night when the words wouldn't surface, his pen frozen, only that vague animal sway inside him.

Come April, he gave in to it. The first day Atigun Pass opened he'd trucked the dogs north up the Dalton. Some four hours later, three thousand miles away, the hammer on Tom Wesley's pistol cocked.

The distance between them, Gavin and Tom Wesley, was greater than the miles: twenty-six years, the old man's funeral the last time the two Dunlap brothers were in the same room, an aged hardness, the fire long gone out of it, only distance now, and cold.

When a neighbor happened over and found Tom Wesley, the blood brown, rindy by then, the body only a hull and ravaged by his disease, black powder burns smudging the pistol barrel, when that neighbor came by, Gavin couldn't have been any farther if he was on the moon, he and the team motoring down the North Slope, the Chevy handling the Dalton like a fly swimming through oatmeal, chassis nodding on spent shocks, load of the sled and eight huskies weighing the rear of the truck down almost into the slush and gravel.

Earlier Gavin had stopped when he reached the pass—that was the very moment he later reckoned Tom Wesley's pistol fired— his truck jibbing in neutral above a world of snow, rock, wind, the Brooks Range unfolding, an east-west run of snaggles and edges, points and slope.

Frosty had yipped, the rest of the boys pressed snouts against wire-mesh cage. What Gavin felt then was his winter twinge, only that.

North, he thought it had said. He let out the brake, white-knuckled the drop, kept driving until fifteen miles beyond the Galbraith Lake pump station, where he parked on a dead-end spur off the Dalton, the pipeline in the distance a snake on the tundra, glinting and infinite.

The dogs smelled the run. Pytka, the handsome five-year-old dun, clown of the bunch, stood, sat, stood, front paws already working, head back, nose up, mouth belling at a milk sky.

Gavin had a word with each. He told his wise dog Clancy of the trip, the caribou, the lead dog regarding Gavin with sleepy eyes.

He tried to explain it, the reason that had brought them up the Dalton, tried to explain the sway that had drawn his bones like gravity all winter.

It was four o'clock, the sun bright, rolling around the circle of the horizon, time to harness. The team pulled, straining at the main and tug lines. He lifted the hook and the sled jumped and they were off, the dogs reaching for snow, no sound except the muffled clack of runners breaking trail.

At seven miles they rounded a hilltop above Atigun Gorge. The dogs bolted—no time to throw the hook, survey a safer descent. The down-rush wasn't much different from skiing Ten Cent Gulch when he was a kid, him and Tom Wesley taking turns strapping on the old man's wood slats, pointing themselves down the hill, T.W. always nervier, always daring Gavin to go like hell. "Oh brother," Tom Wesley'd say after seeing another pittypat run. "You sure you got a pecker in them drawers?"

He was gaining on the dogs now, snow piling over the brush bow, afraid he'd overtake Kenai and Digger. The sled went wide of the team, jerked back behind the line of dogs, went wide, a herringbone path he carved the whole way down.

Camp was in the lee of a snow cornice before a stand of stubbed willows, beyond the brush, a frozen tendril of the Sagavanirktok. At ten o'clock Gavin slid into his bag, the sky still ivory blue. He closed his eyes, thought of night, the winter dark, the January morning the editor from New York called.

"Nothing," he'd said to her when she asked.

"Everybody wants to know," she said. "Gavin Dunlap this. Gavin Dunlap that." Her voice was bristles and spikes. "They all ask. 'Anything new from the Northern Light?' they say." He pictured the dusky office, the smoke. "Everybody," she said. "They ask. For you."

She was young, pretty in a steely way. A wire-haired terrier, she looked to him the only time he'd seen her.

"I was thinking," she said. "A children's book."

The line popped, clicked. He considered how long it had been, shivered at the thought of the last time, how distant, when words were still an engine that could launch him across a page.

"How's that sound?" she said. "Some of those native stories. You know."

"Uh-huh," he said. "Tlingit tales."

"Right."

The static on the line sounded like fire. The editor said something else but Gavin couldn't hear for the interference. In the window his jowly gray face reflected back at him; outside snow was blowing again. He heard the dogs in the kennels, had the same itch the team had, the Coldfoot to Wiseman run.

She said, "It could be anything, really. A story from your own childhood." She waited. "You have a brother, right?"

"No," he said.

"No to the children's book or the brother?"

"No," he said.

That January night, after the run to Wiseman and back, Gavin sensed the pull, the first time. A cankered molar was how it felt, except the feeling didn't come from his mouth but somewhere inside. He thought it was the words finally breaking loose, icebound, all those months of waiting, and he savored its spiky twinge.

And after: He sat with his pen, the dark afternoons.

Yet the tug was wordless, an aurora, a shapeless wild thing, old and submerged as marrow. Three nights running he dreamt of ice, water, scree. Hooves the next night, tracks in snow.

One February morning he found a year-old *Alaska Monthly* in the mudroom, saw an article on the Sagavanirktok, the caribou migration. And Gavin knew then there were hooves running inside him, knew they were running through snow and ice. He thought of the editor in New York, saw the sentences he couldn't write massing on the tundra like herds, caribou moving north.

He couldn't say why but he knew: he had to follow.

THE SECOND DAY ON the Sag the dogs pulled him deeper into the Atigun, four Dall sheep skylighted on a hill all that he saw.

The next day Gavin mushed toward Cloud Peak, wrote verse in the snow with the dogs and sled, only that; no words came. On his way back to camp he saw the first caribou, three of them. His hip was balky from breaking trail. The sweetness, the recognition of those January dreams cut through.

Gavin almost wept at the trio running spidery across the frozen river, their rough poetry. What he saw then in that ice, snow, water, and scree, the hooves in snow, what he saw thrummed, electricity in his nerves firing like caps. It was himself, streaming across a yawning vastness, too, a landscape he couldn't quite see but now understood was as familiar as his bones.

ON THE FOURTH DAY a green apple moisture halo ringed the sun—Gavin read it as an omen, drove the dogs up the Sag toward its headwaters over eighteen miles of ice. He saw more caribou, a herd of twenty, a big bull with flowing beard, the rest following on black spindle legs, a lone calf limping behind. Later another herd. And another.

The morning of the fifth day overflow was running and breakup not far behind, the ice heaved into blue humps the color of sky, snow shrinking, earth and wildberry brambles beginning to patch the tundra like bruises. It was tough going, the boys struggling to break trail.

He saw a herd of five caribou a mile off through willow slash, the caribou circling, running north, the team too tired to chase. Gavin rested the dogs and considered the hoof prints, the yearly migration, the impossibility of all those miles.

The headwaters were up beyond a wrinkle in the horizon, five miles on. They would never make it; the river was turning to water again. He hawed up a side creek, turned the dogs, mushed out the Sag the next day, the tundra more brown than white.

The caribou moved inside him the whole way out. But Gavin was stalled, the winter pull gone slack, that landscape he'd glimpsed only a few days before, the shadows and edges, now black as pitch, again unknown.

It was the right decision, coming out when he did. If the ice had broken up, there was but a thin bench along the lateral moraine that he and the dogs could have sledded, maybe not even that.

Gavin camped off the road on the seventh day, buck-jumped the Chevy over the Dalton back to Coldfoot the next.

The note was on the door. *Call home.* "But I am home," he said. Tom Wesley's body had been on ice for eight days.

What Gavin felt was bone tired. That was all. It was twenty-six years since he'd been back, Tom Wesley twenty-four then, thorny as ever.

"Oh brother," he'd said to Gavin that last time. "Oh brother. The army poet," he'd said, fingering the lapels of Gavin's dress wools. Everybody laughed, Tom Wesley's wife, Maureen, too—this was the evening after the old man was put in the ground, dirt thrown in—nothing left but for T.W. to start up. The battling Dunlap boys, famous all over Trinity, the two as predictable as the deer that swam over the lake twice a year, all hooves and points and beating water.

Tom Wesley had stood there, reedy, hair combed back and thinning, his mouth open, the corners going toward derision, stopping. "The army poet," he said again, quieter, moved on. Later Gavin heard that laugh in the room, sharp, snaking above everybody, certain he was the reason. At one point Maureen buttonholed him, most of the well-wishers already on their way home, the conversation between the two more silence than talk, Gavin already gone himself, three thousand miles away.

He waited at the airstrip for the charter out of Coldfoot, the sky flinty, threatening. He hoped it was enough to weather him in.

He heard it first, a sound irritating as a gnat and no bigger than one when he sighted it. The bush pilot banked, circled the packed snow before landing, the shadow of the plane on the hills. The two didn't bother with talk the whole of the flight to Fairbanks. Gavin watched the land tilt up sideways through the window on takeoff, its Arctic whiteness and vertical crags.

He caught Alaska Air out. After the stopover in Anchorage, a woman took the empty seat next to him. She smelled of lilac and lavender, was thirty-five years maybe, brown hair pulled back into a tail, big rawboned woman. Alaska woman.

After meals were handed out she said, "You have a sadness." A black gap from a missing bicuspid sneaked into her smile.

Gavin wished he'd shaved better, felt sandpaper under his chin. "My brother," he said. "I'm going back for the funeral."

Her face went soft, looked as if her green eyes would leak.

"We weren't close," he said.

She stared at him.

"California," he said, lifting one hand. "Alaska," the other. "Not close at all."

The pilot came on the speaker, talked about Mount Saint Elias, the Malaspina glacier, "bigger than the state of Rhode Island," the pilot said. The woman looked over Gavin's food tray out the window at the rimy mass below.

"You're the Northern Light," she said. "My daughter. She reads you. We must have every one. You're just like the picture on the book." The woman's eyes fixed on him. "I'm Caroline."

"Gavin," he said.

"Of course," she said.

They talked of Alaska, of mud season, guessed when the Nenana ice tripod would fall. She was from Talkeetna, the foot of Denali. "The toenail, actually," she said, laughed, put her hand on his forearm, a ptarmigan alighting, taking off.

"Coldfoot," he said. "The northmost truckstop in the world."

She nudged his knee, said, "What are you working on? Your writing."

Gavin turned to the window, searching the coastline for Yakutat, the Alsek. He thought of caribou, their run across the tundra, equal parts slapstick and ballet, wanted to tell Caroline of their unthinkable migration. He thought of the dreams: ice, water, scree, hooves in snow. He looked back but had no words.

"Full spectrum light," she said. "That's what you need. Full spectrum light. A body up here doesn't get enough," she said. "Winters I walk through greenhouses." She moved closer, lifted the armrest between them, her voice whooshing like the air jet above his head. "Your cells have chromoplasts. You give them full spectrum light and they all line up. It's a fact," she said. "It's what you need."

Gavin chewed at his lip. They didn't talk for some time. Later, during the final descent to Seattle, she said, "Make it right. Your brother." She tapped her chest, said, "I got me a fella who loves me.

I don't need a big career. It's all I need. Love."

He wanted to tell her this was different, wanted to recount the galling history. As the aisle drained he said something else. "The caribou. Every year," he said. "The migration. Amazing." He fell over the words telling her, the wonder, tried to show her with his hands, the mountain steeps, how infinite caribou's range was, their run across ice, legs pedaling almost, like treading water. She stood taller than him by a head, Gavin childlike next to her, red-faced, out of breath.

"I know it," Caroline said, offered him a fiercesome shake. "I used to be a missionary," she said. "Once. A person can be a lot of things in this life."

He thought of her after they went their different directions, she on a connecting flight to the Bay Area. The laser green of her eyes stayed, a glimmering afterimage.

From Seattle Gavin flew to Ashland and from there to Trinity Center in a four-seater charter. On his drive back to the old place he saw two Dunlap Bros. Heating trucks scooting along on 3. He watched each until it rounded a twist in the road, disappeared. Then nothing but road and trees.

GAVIN DIDN'T FIND ANY ghosts in the house, just cold. That and Tom Wesley's ancient Border collie, Spanky. Their old room had been turned into a sewing room for Maureen, never turned into anything else after she'd died six years ago. The rest was pretty much how he remembered it. Their father's chair still by the fire. The kitchen with the oak slab counters stained brown from cooking, rings where pots had branded marks; a roll-away dishwasher now in a corner near the pantry.

There were photos in the hallway, the walls painted white instead of the brown dinge he'd known. A photo of Tom Wesley in his Hayfork football uniform, him smiling like he had cunning to sell. A class picture of Maureen, all thirteen of them, the entire seventh grade, Gavin standing right next to her, the way he did. One of the old man in front of the first Dunlap Heating truck, a prickly sawed-off bantam, head scarcely higher than the radiator cap. The photo of their mother fading, cloud and sepia. "She couldn't pass your big, old head," Tom Wesley had told him when he was nine, his version of how she'd died. "Cut her up but good."

Looking at the pictures, he felt the old battle, saw in his head that night on the pond long ago, Tom and Maureen together, the hellish fight between him and T.W., two fingers broke, blood everywhere, a nose that had never worked the right way since. He turned away and Spanky was there, right behind the bend in his knee, gave him a start. "Good night, nurse," he said to the dog, the black-and-white regarding him with big eyes. "You probably couldn't pull your own weight."

That night he made up the foldaway in the old room, didn't feel comfortable in Tom Wesley and Maureen's room, the pistol on the dresser there, cleaned up shiny as when it was his father's. The old man, he'd hold it up to the light. "Boys," he'd say, "now, this here's a sidearm." Gavin and his brother would watch him, try to imagine the significance of such a thing.

It was a night of fitful sleep in the room, everything catching up with Gavin. Fifty was too young to die, he thought, even if it was Tom Wesley. Lying in bed, he considered the two-year difference in their ages, the vast distance, wider than any horizon he could ever imagine as a kid.

Back then he'd lie awake nights in this room, thinking about it, the door shut against his father, Tom Wesley sleeping. At eight he'd resolved to somehow catch his brother up, as if the two of them were both jalopies and he could pull alongside, ride through life dead even with Tom Wesley after that.

Gavin almost told his brother one night what a good life that would be, the two of them even-steven, seeing the world. The old man had beat Tom Wesley for some fool thing, beat him until blood was coming from his ear. He could hear his brother's crying that night in bed, his clogged breathing. Gavin wanted to say something, offer up a salve for the blows.

But then he remembered: he was the good son, Tom Wesley not. And the little room cleaved as if in two and the words never got feet under them to travel across it. He lay in bed that night, the dark of the room coarse as wool, and just listened to the bubbles in his brother's breathing.

GAVIN WOKE TO THE phone ringing and Spanky on his chest. It was Wendell Patton on the line, from the mortuary.

"We were thinking of two days from now," Wendell said. "Give you the time to put things in order."

Gavin said, "Fine." He looked out the window. The backyard had gone to seed, grass growing up over the old red pump. Two sides of the barn were down, the sun coming over it, dogwoods starting to bud. He saw how the Jeffrey pine stooped now, limbs lopped off, probably dying.

"It's a terrible loss," Wendell said.

Gavin shooed Spanky off him, considered how hungry he was. His last meal was on the plane.

"We're having a memorial," Wendell said. "A wake, really. Tomorrow night. The Northfork Grange." His voice was stubble rough. "Should be a good turnout. The old gang. Jinx Hardy. You remember Jinx."

Gavin closed his eyes, remembered. He saw a face dagger thin.

It was right out back Tom Wesley and Jinx had tied him down by the pump, dropped carpenter ants, one by one, on Gavin's stomach, watched the welts rise. "This is rich," Tom Wesley'd said. "Oh brother." Jinx laughed like air coming out of a tire.

Wendell said now, "We're hoping you can say something. A few words."

Gavin sat up, pulled the sheet off him. He felt the bar from the foldaway on his back. "I wouldn't know what," he said.

"He was your brother," Wendell said.

"It's been so long," he said. "The last few years. Can you tell me anything?"

"He was lonely. After Maureen, her cancer."

Gavin tried to picture it, couldn't. All he saw was a twenty-four-year-old Tom Wesley, hair raked back, squibbed mouth, the laugh.

Wendell said, "He talked of you all the time. Very proud."

They were trained to do this, Gavin thought, be solicitous.

"The Grange," Wendell said. "Eight o'clock."

LATE MORNING, GAVIN DROVE through Hayfork. He had to get out, felt himself drawn from the house. It wasn't the winter pull. The caribou, the North Slope tundra, the boys on the Sag, the wordless thing that had held him since January—all of it now seemed so far away. "It's foolishness," he said to Spanky on the car seat next to him, "me giving a speech. Foolish."

The wipers scraped the windshield. Early May, still winter raw, skies steel, holding water. He had to remind himself he wasn't back in the Interior, the trees shaking in a wind that might have followed the tailfin of the plane, all the way from the Gulf of Alaska.

"Twenty-six years," he said. The black-and-white watched him. It groaned, lay down, rolled over onto its back.

"Look at me," Gavin said, "talking to this dog."

The high school was different, the old brick replaced by glass and angles, the concrete stands of the stadium dozed for green stamped metal. On the field he threw a chewed-up ball to the dog. After half an hour, he walked behind the stand of pines, down the grade on the other side of the field.

The dredger pond was the same. The rocks were still piled from the old mining operation, mounds of them, a deep pond where the land creased.

Gavin told the dog about the trip, the frozen Sag. "I got me eight dogs," he said. "They're good boys. Bred to run." He described the quiet of the valley, told Spanky about the fourth day when the team came across the dead caribou's rib cage, the tug lines almost tied into knots from their excitement, snow thick in the canyon, ice lucent as mirrors, the promise of the headwaters still alive, ahead in a cradle of the Philip Smith Mountains.

Spanky didn't care about the tundra, the caribou, only the ball. Gavin tried to think of what to say at the Grange tomorrow but only remembered the night at the dredger pond years ago, Maureen and Tom Wesley on the ice.

Hours later he still couldn't think of anything to say about Tom Wesley. Before the words had gotten locked up, writing had always been one more way for him to run, each page another horizon, white, untracked as snow. Now it was the words doing the fleeing.

He'd run to the army first. Fort Bragg was never far enough from Trinity, never enough to shake the memories of the house, the drill sergeant a pale shadow of his father, all strut and spleen. The fight had kept coming to Gavin, bad dreams of his last year of living in Trinity, the old man and his grain alcohol, Tom Wesley and Maureen.

Tom Wesley'd been working for the company a year by the fall of Gavin's senior year in high school. It was a terrible time, their father getting into his cups earlier and earlier, thin as heating pipe by then, old and bent. Fortified by a lunchtime tootful, he rode Tom Wesley like a mustang every afternoon at work, trying to break his spirit into a hundred pieces. His drunk deepened after he got home. The old man in the chair with his glass, not even getting up to go to the bathroom these days, just hobbling over to the window.

But Tom Wesley, it didn't seem like anything or anyone could sink him. He was earning money, had clothes, a new sea-green Impala he had the privilege of making payments on. All over high school there was the talk of Tom Wesley and Jinx roaring through the county, the girls whispering, cutting their eyes when they talked of the escapades.

Gavin had tried to fill the outsized dimensions of his big brother, went out for football but couldn't take the licks and quit. After that he walked Maureen home on school-day afternoons, same as ever, the crunch of shoulder pads fading into the fall air, the wet of the season. He talked about what was to be, places he'd like to go, this new state Alaska. He'd always thought she'd understood: he was speaking for the two of them.

Nights Gavin escaped the old man's fire by retreating to the barn, did his homework by lantern light, and after the lessons were done, he started in on his writings. The words stumbled worse than his father, but sitting in that drafty barn, the cat chasing mice, itch of chaff in the air, he knew the words could take him somewhere much farther than Tom Wesley's Impala. Sometimes when he saw the light go out by the old man's chair, Gavin went walking, still full of words, walked the three miles to Maureen's and looked up at her window.

Tom Wesley and Maureen was the last thing he could have suspected. His brother never paid her any mind in all of his nineteen years. It just seemed to be Jinx and him those nights, the Impala easing in the drive sometime after midnight, the old man knocked out from the liquor, Gavin still out in the barn with his pad, Tom Wesley sneaking in the house, flicking a cigarette on the walkway, and, once in the house, sending his own stream out the window.

THE WEATHER TURNED AND it snowed in the Trinities the night of Tom Wesley's memorial at the Grange. The drive was squirrelly, Big Creek Road unplowed, slick.

He was a half hour late in arriving, a sizable crowd already inside, the voices going soft as nap when he entered. On one side of the room, the one with the long wall of shoulder-high tongue and groove, a bar. Opposite that, a series of bay windows, the curtains yellowed, drawn. In the corner near the far wall, a poster-sized photo on an easel.

Gavin still hadn't decided on anything to say, felt the eyes on him, a hundred pinpoints. He stamped the snow from his feet, busied himself with hanging his coat, conversations starting up again in the room, filling the hollow he'd created when he'd opened the door, them seeing who it was.

The corner near the easel was empty and that was where Gavin went. It took a minute for him to recognize who it was in the picture. A gray man, hair mostly gone, no spark or wile on his face, only a brush of a mustache. It was Tom Wesley.

It gave him a start when he realized it. All these years, twenty-six of them, the time he was north, all that time he'd carried a far different image: Tom Wesley, firstborn, the battling Dunlap boy who fought, won, had the company to show for it, the old man's silver-plated six-gun, Maureen; Tom Wesley, riding life like it was his very own pony.

But this was not that face, affliction sorrowing the eyes, the folds and wrinkles that could hold a month of rain. An old man, was all. It was a face that said it was life that was doing the riding in those twenty-six years. And Gavin lost himself in that stranger in the picture, had a flurry in his stomach, not reward, not sobersidedness, but an unmooring of surprise, discovery. And he was alone there, the noise in the hall no more than wind.

"Gavin?" A rusty voice from behind him. He turned to a doughy, squat man, eyeglasses the color of carbon, a square head. "I don't expect you'd remember me," the man said. "Wendell Patton."

They shook, talked about the arrangements, the car that would pick him up tomorrow. "You look like you could do with a drink," Wendell said.

Gavin's throat was patchy with the idea of his speech later, saying the words he still couldn't think of. "I could that," he said. "A drink."

Room was made at the bar, a handful of ragtag faces, respectful. Wendell introduced the knot of them, Gavin repeating the names, forgetting moments later; he was only good with dogs, knew every last one in Coldfoot.

They spouted their sorries, a gentle rain. He winced, held up his hand, a gesture of admitting and accepting but stoppering up, too, their kindnesses.

"A devil of a time tracking you down," said a woman with dull brown hair, hardly any eyebrows at all, only two lines on a shiny face.

Gavin drank the bourbon, it igniting his throat, staying lit inside him. He smiled, looked not quite level into her eyes. "I was out with my dogs," he said. "Above the Arctic Circle. Mushing."

The one with Jess stitched in script over his pocket whistled, said, "The truth?"

Gavin nodded. Another bourbon replaced the first.

Jess said, "Don't that beat all." The group hummed with amazement at such a thing, Gavin and his dogs.

"How many you got?" said Shiny Face.

"I got eight dogs," he said. "Uh-huh. Eight." He twirled a coaster on the cherrywood.

A fellow with red suspenders edged forward, gut spilling over his pants, black and gray stirrup sideburns. "What's the cost to feed that mess?"

Gavin said, "A ton of food lasts four months. That's twelve hundred and eighty-six dollars for the food and two hundred and ninety yet for the postage."

They laughed at the thought of so much kibble. Red Suspenders asked about rearing huskies, training them. Gavin told of tying a log to a three-month-old pup, getting it used to the harness, hitching eight-month-olds to the sled with a seasoned dog. He drank the bourbon. "If they have a bad experience the first time out, they never take to it," he said. "Just don't."

After a few more questions, the talk of mushing stalled. Gavin busied himself with another bourbon, the faces around him, shy smiles, them looking down at the floor, some weepy country music in the background.

Somebody pushed through. "I bet you don't remember me," he said. His face was fat, hair long on one side and combed over the top. "Jinx Hardy," he said. "Told you." His laugh was an animal panting.

The knot grew, more people pressing in to see the brother from

Alaska who'd come home to bury Tom Wesley. He saw the expectation, the need of theirs to give sanctification to that body that'd been on ice ten days now. He saw it and it snagged him like a tooth, Gavin caught on all the possible things the strange face on the easel could mean to these people.

A woman thin as a rake leaned in, black hair piled high, stamp of splotchy lipstick slightly out of register. "I was the one who found him," she said.

"I'm sorry," Gavin said.

"It wasn't much of a mess," she said. "Just the back of his head." She waved her hand at the memory.

"A good man," Red Suspenders said.

"He had a real gentleness in him," Shiny Face said. "Inside him. It was there. Inside."

Jinx stabbed his finger in the air, spittle flecking the corners of his fleshy mouth. "He and Maureen," he said. "They couldn't have any kids. I guess you knew that. Broke their hearts."

Gavin nodded. He didn't know. Their story, Tom Wesley and Maureen's, had ended after the old man went.

"Of course, he could be a difficult bastard," Jinx said. A faint smile played on his lips. "Guess you knew that also. But to Maureen he never was, not once." He told how compassionate he'd been toward her, especially at the end. Gavin sipped his whisky, a small fire in his stomach, watched that broad face move up and down.

Wendell said, "You did him proud."

"Always bragging on you," Jinx said. "How you got away. Escaped the old man."

"The poetry, too," Wendell said.

Gavin nodded, tried to fit everything they were saying into his head but it kept falling out, only the whisky filling him up, smoldering.

"Had us frame one right up here in the Grange," Jess said.

Gavin looked at what he was pointing at behind the bar, saw it was his poem "Wild Night" from his first book under glass.

"Pretty good," Jess said. "You got any verse that rhymes?"

Gavin laughed, shoved his hands under the bar-top, embarrassed by his skinny repute.

Jinx said, "He was always making us recite it. 'My brother,' T.W. would say, 'conquering the north,' he'd say."

"A regular pistol," Red Suspenders said, then went ashen, looked as if he'd swallowed lye. He shook his head. "Sorry. But he was. A pistol."

The crowd had grown around Gavin, the people eager to tell him of his brother. It was a strange thing for him, the whisky unloosed inside him by now, three or four shots of it, his ill blood tapped, wild, leaving tracks in a landscape that had been frozen for twenty-six years.

The back of Gavin's neck prickled. This person they were telling him of, this gray man in the photo—it wasn't Tom Wesley, not the one he knew. He thought of a thousand other stories, different ones, all their sharp points of antagonism, pieces of another life.

"Just the week before he—" Red Suspenders said, paused, scratched the back of his head. "Just before, you know." He held both hands up to fill in the rest, the shooting. "We'd talked about hunting deer one more time. Once they come back over the lake. The disease was pretty far along. He seemed to perk at the notion, though."

Wendell said, "A tragedy. Everyone thought the pain at first was just bursitis, a pinched nerve."

"That was back in January," Jinx said.

He thought of his own January: the call from the editor in New

York, the mush to Wiseman and back, the dark afternoons, his pull, deep inside, a tidal draw. All that time, Tom Wesley's life was slipping through dead hands; nerves going extinct; everything he had or was, slackening: his brother scared.

It was a picture as unlikely as the one in the corner of that Grange hall. What Gavin saw instead was white and cold and winter dark, a night from thirty years ago. Maureen had told him of the date, the ice skating. He'd asked Tom Wesley outright. "Sure," his brother had said, flicking hair out of his eyes, one side of his mouth pulled up, a slingshot. "Why in hell would she want you there," he'd said, standing over Gavin, "to write poetry?"

He'd gone anyway, watched from the hill. Tom Wesley and Maureen, Jinx and Jane Ann Birdwell, their tracks down through snowdrifts to the dredger pond, across rock heaps, their blades etching ice. He couldn't hear, only see — the two couples skating hand-in-hand, later forming a whip, cracking it, snapping the end skater across the pond. Even later, when Tom Wesley had taken a hatchet to the ice, Jinx off to the side drinking from a bottle. Then his brother's clothes came off, skivvies, too, and he'd jumped in. Maureen and Jane Ann doubled over, laughing at the sight of it; Gavin heard that all the way up the hill, like chimes. Tom Wesley treaded the black water, then shinned out. And Maureen, she hugged him to her, his brother red, raw.

Wendell said now, "He was an honorable man. Bore it as best he could."

All those faces nodded.

Gavin only saw the ice on that pond and then heard himself, voice tight, saying, "He couldn't take it."

The woman with the big hair, the one who'd found Tom Wesley, huffed, her mouth open, lipstick nicking her teeth like blood.

"He couldn't take it," he said again, his face now hot, his loudness surprising him. What he heard gave a jolt. It wasn't his voice but his father's, that cruel, pinched whisky voice. "Death," the voice said. "Where I live, people don't go running from it. Alaska." He saw eyes on him, the air gray with smoke, all those eyes black and small as punctuation marks. "Bill Benson," Gavin said. "Bush pilot. Came to grief in the Anaktuvuk. He made one big tinfoil ball, he did." Gavin showed them with his hands, his left, the airplane, smashing into his right hand, the mountain. "Slim Jim Mackey," he said. "Froze to death on his snow machine. Rode out one December day, never came back."

And Gavin saw that this was what he had to say for Tom Wesley, only this. And he let the old man do the talking. He told of the Reeves brothers, Arnie Goldsmith, Eustice Dale. "Moose stomped old Eustice," he said, the whisky boiling in him now. "Each and every one," he said. "Bigger men. My brother?" He shook his head. "He couldn't take it."

Jinx stepped forward, the little nib of his jaw almost lost in wattle and fat. "Now, see here," he said. "You're brothers."

Gavin looked at him, tried to find the boy who laughed like air coming out of a tire, Tom Wesley's partner in crime. The faces before him—suspicion shading them, closing up, the room dim as twilight.

"That battle of yours not quit yet?" Jinx said. "Gavin, the old boy is dead."

Gavin gripped the shot glass on the bar, felt it dig into wood, the hurly-burly of the hall swimming in his head, people hemming him in, all those stone-hard faces, their hearts filled with Tom Wesley.

It wasn't much of a fight, wasn't much of anything. Gavin pushed Jinx. That was all. He swung a haymaker but only hit air.

The crowd made a sound, voices on a carnival ride, a *whoooo* dissolving into the smoke and gloaming.

He tried to shake off Wendell and Jess. They were hurrying him out of the hall, into the sleety night. Once home he didn't remember the drive back along Big Creek Road. He sat with Spanky on the foldaway, his drunk now queasiness. And he carried on the argument with himself, falling asleep as he kicked it around, that it was *he* who was the good brother, not Tom Wesley. Him.

IT WOULD ONLY BE a short while until he'd be back in Coldfoot. That was what Gavin told himself when he woke the next day, Tom Wesley's funeral. He couldn't picture much of the night before, only whisky heat.

Spanky watched him, eyes big as quarters. He sat with the dog, waiting for the car from the mortuary, his head smarting from last night's drunk.

The house was oppressive, all that weight. *Dead* weight. He was the last—the rest gone—the last of the battling Dunlap boys.

"I know," he said to the black-and-white. "A sad thing for you." The dog's eyes were sleep-caked. "He was," Gavin said and stopped, considering the gray stranger he'd seen for the first time last night. He mulled over what to say. "He was good to you," he said finally.

Wendell knocked a few minutes shy of nine-thirty. There was a mouse under one lens of his glasses, the bruise yellow, blue, brown.

Gavin didn't remember that. "I'm sorry," he said, a sourness in his stomach. "Last night."

"We all handle death differently," Wendell said, hands up in supplication, his mortuary pitch.

"I want to take him along," Gavin said, pointing to the dog. "The funeral."

Wendell cocked his head.

"It was his dog," Gavin said.

He and Spanky rode in the back of the car, Wendell driving in front of the smoked plate glass. At the mortuary, the other cars fell in line, Gavin's car behind the hearse, the rest of the cortege with headlights glowing.

It was a handsome day, the May snow still white and lining the road, spring retaking the rest. He rolled down the window and Spanky stuck his head out. Gavin had forgotten the green Trinity mornings, the smell of pine, sharp and clean. A jaundiced sun hung in the sky—he remembered the woman on the flight from Anchorage, her name he couldn't recall, the mumbo jumbo she said about sunlight he could.

After fifteen miles on 3 the lake unfurled. Spanky sniffed at the water and firs, Gavin holding the dog by its collar. He didn't see the hearse stop when it did. And when he did see it, he thought that it had stalled out.

Wendell pulled up alongside. Gavin got out of the car, saw then the fish and game truck fifty yards off, the orange cones on the road.

"Problem?" he said.

"The deer," Wendell said, pointing. "They're back."

Gavin could see them, far off, necks straining above the algid water on their spring migration across the lake, legs bicycling, comical almost, the herd swimming across that impossible distance.

Watching them grow from specks to animals in their crossing took a good while. The caribou ran through him. But what hung in mind, ultimately, was not the herds and tundra. It was Tom Wesley, that and a spasm of shame. How far it was Tom Wesley had come, a scabrous bully all his little brother had ever known. The rest, the gray man on the easel whom Hayfork knew, loved—that was an invisible terrain to Gavin. He'd only seen edges and shadows, an occasional Christmas card—*Gavin Dunlap's going to the dogs!*—nothing more.

The last few steps of that migration Tom Wesley had taken alone, baby steps. Every day the disease had chipped away at who he'd become until in the end he couldn't even lift his arms to fight if he'd wanted.

The deer were nearly across the lake now, windmilling legs. It was a wondrous thing. And inside Gavin a string pulled tight, that indefinable winter tug returning again. Only now he could see what was attached on the other end: a trapdoor that spilled open. And then the words finally came.

"Oh brother," he said. "Tom Wesley," he said. That was all.

The deer regained their grace, scrabbled out of the water, puncturing the thin apron of ice, hooves clattering over shale and snow crust, then up the hill, across 3, into the woods.

Trapline

DELMONT NEALE WAS A big, beautiful man right up to the end, the day his 4x4 went off the road, spilling the bobcat pelts onto Highway 3. He was unlike any man I ever knew. From our first days together in the navy at Mare Island over twenty years ago, when he walked past my bunk looking like he was put together not with skin and bone but armor, the cheek lines on his face so sharp they must have been cut by a diamond saw, something in me changed.

I didn't know what love was then. I didn't even know what I was. And when I finally did, I didn't ever tell Delmont. He never suspected.

Nobody in the county does. It's not strange for a middle-aged man in Trinity County to be unattached. There aren't too many people here, only a few thousand, and what people there are, a good number are drunks and crankheads. A lot of the rest get lost in the land. It's so big here, it fills them up. They simply can't fit someone else in their lives.

Most people probably think I'm lost that way. I'm the fish

and game warden. A funny thing that. My public life is anything
but wild.

There are enough black bears and cougars and eight-point
bucks and red-tailed hawks for all my days. That's Trinity County:
not a stoplight in the whole of the place, not a properly incorpo-
rated town in the handful of crossroads that took root under its
trees. That's what it is. Trees and animals and lakes and rivers and
hills and a few thousand people.

But a wild life, no.

Despite its bigness — the place is about the size of
Connecticut — the people are small. Alternative lifestyle means
living at a campground. Butch is a kind of wax for hair or mustache. And so on.

I'M GOOD AT HOLDING things inside. My breath, for example.
In the navy, I could make a scuba tank last longer than any other
gob in the whole company. It's still probably a record.

That's actually how I met Delmont, holding my breath. When
I stretched the tank to its absolute limits in the training pool, he
came up to me afterward in the locker room, snapped a towel at
me. "What do you have, gills or something? That's not human. You
must be some kind of fish," he said.

A week ago, I hyperventilated, slid down into the bathwater,
stayed down until my lungs were burning, nearly exploding, the
phosphors jiggering in front of my eyes, and then I burst from the
water like some primordial beast. Over two and a half minutes I
clocked in at. I still have it.

When my breathing rounded out to normal and the water
settled again in the tub, I thought of Delmont in the bottom of
Stuart Fork.

The water was a riot that first day after the accident. It looked like the mountain range on the relief map in my office, raised and white and brown, except it was always moving, reforming. And it sounded like a demolition derby, the noise of the runoff moving boulders downstream.

Nobody had even actually seen the truck at that point, the water was so crazy. But I knew he was down there; I didn't need to see the Dodge to know. I knew from the pelts.

When Delmont pitched in he would have had a small air bubble in the top of the truck cab, a supply that would have lasted maybe twenty minutes. In the end, he would have been pressing his face to the roof, sucking the last bits of the air, then his world would have gone to shadows, then night, darker yet than his poor heart.

I'VE GONE TO STUART FORK every day since. The season has brought storm after storm and the waters have risen, the creek becoming an exaggeration of itself. And old Delmont, he's been suspended in some unholy place between life and death, his body not recovered. Of course, there are questions surrounding everything. I get a call every other day from the sheriff about the bobcats.

That first day when I got the call I drove out immediately. The snow had turned more to an icy rain. I didn't want to think about it, the freezing chowder of snow and sleet and rain from the night before, Delmont's 4x4 cartwheeling end over end and into Stuart Fork like a drunken high-school cheerleader. It was rain on my face, I told myself, not tears. I half expected to see his head break the surface of the water, cheeks puffed with air, eyes bugging from holding his breath for so long, mustache wet and droopy and looking like the legs of a centipede. "What you looking at?" Then that laugh of his.

But the only thing that broke the surface of the water was more water. The creek ran fat and obscene, a racing engine. I couldn't get a good read.

The accident, the disappearing truck, the pelts, all of it was just like Delmont. For the slimmest of moments I thought maybe this was another of his stunts. That was the thing with him: you never knew.

IT IS AMAZING WHAT some animals can do to survive. Adaptability. If a link in the food chain is broken, the animal manufactures another link. Last summer, for example, when mountain lion prey thinned out. In Hoopa, a woman opened the door to her back porch and saw her pet potbelly pig in the jaws of a cougar. I was called in but there was nothing I could do. I told her for all the rules I have to enforce in my job, I couldn't regulate nature.

That might seem somewhat surprising coming from me. After all, I've survived as long as I have up here by living by the rules, within straight lines and tidy borders, regulating my nature. But every month, I get the itch for something less tame, a twang of wildness running through me, a need to let out what's inside me and put my jaws into something, and I drive the hundred miles to Eureka. After Junction City, 299 turns sinuous, coiling like a tail, and I shed who everybody thinks I am before reaching the Humboldt County line.

I turn into a hunter. I go to the certain bars I know, I prowl, seek out the company that's there. The next day on my way home, my old self is always waiting for me by the side of the road, a familiar ghost, and I slip back into it like it's a uniform.

The other way I've survived was Delmont Neale. After we were discharged eighteen years ago, I followed him to the county just before he and Patsy got married. I was the best man. Imagine that.

What I loved in Delmont was his wildness. He wasn't, in the horse sense of the word, ever properly broken. For all the rigid borders I saw in county society, how I was supposed to act and be, all he saw was blurred and smirchy. He cultivated marijuana plants right there at the tree farm. If you were angling for a certain car or gun or generator, anything, it was only a matter of asking.

And then there was the poaching.

SOMETHING HAPPENED A WEEK and a half ago when I was at Stuart Fork. I saw something new in the water: blue returning to the edges, then something deeper in the white center, a flash of red, then nothing, then another flash of it, then I saw it, the waggling shape of Delmont's Dodge under the rapids.

It hit me. The thought of him down at creek bottom, distended from water, air still trapped in his body—I know what a body looks like that's been under for that long. I couldn't stay there, drove off to the trapline for the first time since the accident.

My snowshoes broke the drifts, barked with each step. I looked for tracks on the trail but there weren't any. Our trapline is in a wide bowl of a canyon, the firs and oaks and pines fanning back in some arboreal agreement forming an egg-shaped meadow, a place only we knew. Above the ridgeline the sun was deciding whether to shine or hide. The wind came chuffing down the hill.

Here's the curious thing. At the trapline, the chains were pulled tight on the stakes, the traps, all five of them, sprung. And what I found after pushing the mounds of snow off almost knocked me over.

Locked in the jaws were stuffed toy animals: a bear, a cougar, a beaver, a fox, a wolf. The cougar had reddish dye on it, the color of blood. *Murder* was written on the wolf with the dye.

Every year there were stories about the environmentalists. But this canyon, it doesn't exist, is five miles off any marked trail. Only Delmont and I knew about it. I couldn't explain it.

Then I did something else I couldn't explain. I rebaited the trapline. After all that had happened, the accident, what they found at the roadside, it didn't make any sense. Just the same, I pulled back the jaws on those clanking, serrated iron beasts—not offset and padded according to the regulations spelled out in all the manuals in my office—balled up the meat I'd brought, rescented the area.

"LIFE DON'T MEASURE UP to any rule," Delmont liked to say. I would have to agree. The slow, solitary drip of my life is filled with the numbing detail of licenses and tags and fines. But underneath all that I'm a wild man. The season for bobcat runs from November 24 to January 31; Delmont's accident was February 18; I rebaited the traps on March 3.

I draw the line for everybody else. Then I step over it.

I know there's no reasonable explanation for it. In the past, an adult winter pelt would get $250, easy. In a good year, with some luck and a crafty line, we'd catch sixty to seventy pelts. You can add up the take yourself.

But there's no market for bobcat anymore. "The environmentalists," I told Delmont. "People's tastes change." Still we kept the line going.

For Delmont, the charm was like a game of chicken. He needed to know how far he could take it. It was something to do.

For me, it was something to do *with him*, better yet a secret, something that's held deep below the surface, goes all the way down to one's center.

Even in a place as uncivilized as the county, people like to think society is something that raises us above the animals. I know different. Way down, where the secrets are, it's anarchy, no rules or rhyme or reason to what one really is. That's nature; it's base and hungry and ultimately undeniable. No wonder a lot of people up here have religion. Faced with it all, living so close to something so big, they feel nearer to God. They think He's a full-time resident in the county. It must be comforting to believe there's some kind of greater plan, scary and too unsettling to think otherwise.

A little church in Coffee Creek captures this spirit. Set back in a stand of sugar pines and white firs, it has a blue tin roof so faded by weather it looks like an approximation of heaven. Out front, below the sign announcing weekly services beginning on Sundays at ten A.M., is another sign with a message routed in it. YOU ARE NOT YOUR OWN, it says.

Yesterday I passed the church going to visit Delmont at Stuart Fork and it made me smile. "All right, whose am I?" I said alone in my truck cab, the question of my life.

All the same, I know the message the sign intends. It's saying we're all a part of something bigger, far bigger than this place even.

I think you can read it differently. That you're not bigger than yourself, can't burst the bubble of you that's way down deep. That's the place you really draw from. You breathe from the inside out.

SPRING IS COMING. EVER since Delmont's Dodge came hovering into view, there's been more talk about putting the hooks on his truck and drawing it out. It feels like a long time since he went in.

Most of the dots have now been connected. Not the pelts yet. People, knowing Delmont's thieving ways, are no doubt assuming the worst.

I have my own version of what happened to Delmont. I'd like to think that somewhere between hitting the deer and going into Stuart Fork he said what he always did after staring down the barrel of harm's way: "I showed them how the cow ate the cabbage." Maybe, too, he thought of me.

Squirting around the road like a raddled bottle rocket, he had two, maybe three seconds. Of course, he couldn't have said what I hoped he did. Just like in the more than twenty years I had with him, I couldn't ever say what I wanted, never had the right time. Instead of opening my mouth, I swallowed, pushed down what I was so I could be with him.

I WENT BACK TO the trapline yesterday for the first time since the stuffed animals. The snow had melted some, the brown showing through, and I tramped the distance without my snowshoes. The traps were empty, slack on their chains. The season for winter pelts would be over soon.

Freshening the bait and scenting the traps, I remembered a story Delmont told me a few years back. He had a full sack of pelts, had almost come out of the woods, five miles out of the canyon and not more than a quarter mile from his truck, when he heard voices and lay flat in the snow. He was close enough, not twenty yards from them, to identify who they were, the district ranger and someone else, I've forgotten who, from the forest service. And he lay there, hiding, hugging the sack, night coming down, scarcely breathing until they passed him by and drove off.

There was a light deep in his eyes when he told me. The brush with being discovered excited the reckless streak inside him. I felt it, too, when he told me. And I knew exactly what it was. That delicious, spiky tension that teeter-totters between capturing and getting caught.

Me, I didn't have that keen sense of free fall yesterday. It was something other than wildness I felt. I knew, standing in the clearing of the canyon, why I'd come, what I was looking for. It wasn't for bobcats, not even animals, not real ones. It was for stuffed animals. And when I saw the traps still yawning open, the five of them empty, I felt something snap on me: a conclusion I'd been nearing, the sense I was the game being caught.

Maybe it was Delmont: the trapline and the stuffed animals. Maybe it was he who planted them, his funny way of telling me he knew all along. I lie awake nights thinking about it, the hiss and hammer of my radiator keeping time. In those dark moments I get the uneasy feeling that perhaps I didn't cover my tracks as well as I thought. Who's to say? Delmont's not talking any.

I hear they're going to put the hooks in his 4x4 any day now, winch it up like it's some dead carcass. When they do, it will pitch and yaw in the current, his dead eyes remaining unblinking as they raise the whole shooting match from the bottom. And the last bubbles, finally dislodged, will climb and explode on the surface like untold secrets.

May

MAY HAD GONE ALL draggle-tailed working the drift. Swinging an eight-pound pickax seven hours on end will do that. It didn't matter that the mercury was edging toward the skinny side of forty degrees, it being early November. Hardscrabbling would get the sweat running like sap.

"Getting close, Gruff," she said. "I can feel it. That vein's going to rise like—what'd you always call it?—a varicose vein." Nobody else was in there with her. In her head, hell yes, Gruff was there. But stooping in this crosscut of the abandoned Jubilee Mine, it was only May, a pickax, a rusty wheelbarrow, the rest of her hand tools.

She'd been that way, rickety-headed, for some time, over two years the best she could make out, maybe more. Whatever she could excavate from inside her head, she'd done already, and mostly what she found was more gray than gold, the walls too thick to penetrate any further.

She knew there was the man and the little girl, her husband and daughter she took them to be. Sometimes the picture came in clearer, like she had fiddled with a set of rabbit ears, but they never got any more real than dreams, shadows.

They were about as good to her now as pyrite anyway, if they weren't some other trick of her mind. If they actually were real—that was another life. She could remember as far back as two and a half years ago, the day she stepped out of the swollen river, the rapids running crazy, she covered in blood and mucus like a new-born, but no more. Two weeks later was when she became May.

"You know what I could do with right now? Some AN-FO cartridges, Gruff," she said, though she knew she was just saying that. May didn't want the forest service to get wind of her being in the old Jubilee because she had no claim to it. A charge would just as likely set them off as loosen the hard rock overburden. No, her pickax and hand tools would do just fine, thanks.

She knew soon, in a few weeks probably, the rock would get too hard to work with any kind of tool—jackhammer, stoper, drifter, what have you. And she'd have to close out for the season.

By then, the hills around Boulder Creek would be thick with bear hunters, their packs of hellhounds running until they treed a bear or dropped, the hunters acting no better, usually worse, greasy from skinning hides and lit up from drink, full of noisy animal lust at the Goldfield campground, reliving the kill in the cold nights outside their tents until they themselves dropped.

May swung the pickax, smoothed the wall face, swung again. Deep inside the adit, a nostril in the rise of decomposed granite, she could feel night coming on. "It's just a matter of time, Gruff," she said. "I've sent out my twenty letters. That vein's going to rise."

And she thought about what that faint glimmer in the wall, catching, bouncing the light from her lantern, would look like. Three more swings of the pickax and she lay it down, shoveled the waste rock into the wheelbarrow, resealed the adit with the board, and walked the two hundred yards to her blue two-man tent at Goldfield.

MAY HAD LATCHED ON with Gruff north of here, two weeks after picking herself up out of the river, after being vomited into the shallows and hitching rides south from the Cascades through Oregon and into Klamath, her ears still ringing with the sucking sounds of the rapids, the yelling of the water.

She was wandering 96 looking like a lost calf when Murphy's Dodge drove by, stopped, and backed up. What a sight she was! Still undone from slamming through the oxbows, she had one shoe on, the other foot, her right, filthy and bloody and bare; her pants were torn every which way; her shirt raggedy to just this side of decency, the purple bruises on her upper arm starting to yellow.

Murphy leaned out the cab and said, "You look like you were rode hard and put away wet."

Palmer elbowed him, stopping Murphy's smile before it grew any, Palmer being the Christian one of the lot. "What's your name?" Palmer said.

She worked on this while the Dodge shook there roadside in neutral, thinking as far back as she could. She heard the river's voice, was locked once again in its frigid womb, and shivered the way the stoper did if you didn't grip down real firm on its handles. The man and the girl washed through her head briefly but sank. And after all that, she had no answer.

"Where you coming from?" Palmer asked gently, interrupting her vision of spray, rocks, and sky.

North, she pointed.

"You want a job?"

She nodded slowly.

"Here." Palmer passed a pair of coveralls out the window to her. "Climb in back."

She first saw Gruff then, sitting in the pickup bed with the caps and cartridges, air cylinder, hand tools, jackhammer, the rest of their sorry equipment. Even with him sitting back on his haunches, he was an enormous sight—a body that was more a small hill than a body, a face lined like puzzle bark. They didn't say anything on the ride to Lucky Boy. Later when she passed him carting out tailings, he said, "Careful. Mind that jackleg, girlie," and she did.

Back at the truck at day's end, Gruff squinted at her, pinching his face up. He looked over toward the claim, then Murphy and Palmer fooling with the air cylinder. "Goddamn, you believe it's May already," he said to nobody in particular and returned to trying to make what he could of her, taking her in with eyes that looked like water. "So what's your name, honey?"

She thought again. "It's May," she said, deciding finally.

"Mine's Griffin." His voice was full of rasps and nails and she thought of him as Gruff after that.

May bunked in Gruff's shack at Horse Creek while they worked Lucky Boy because he said she could and because she had no other place to stay. Over the summer she turned as hard as the rock walls lining the tunnel, the fat from who she was before disappearing, sloughing off seemingly every day like the loosened overburden she carted out of the stope. And in time she fully became May.

IT WAS TOLERABLE LIVING with Gruff. The shack was small but the beds were separate and he wasn't interested in coupling. Once in the beginning he tried to take her from behind but it wasn't with much spirit and she didn't think he worked right, had no steel in him, and he never tried again.

Most nights after they shook the rock dust from themselves and cleaned up, they sat out front of the shack on the planks he called his deck.

He told her a little about himself, that there was trouble in his past, some jail for boosting construction tools at a job he was working, problems with liquor. At night when he talked in the dark he looked more bear than man, sounded it, too, his voice growling.

May understood how a mind could flood, how it could run wild. She knew about darkness, though she didn't tell him about the river. And what was there to tell? He knew everything about her since she became May, and whatever happened before, she couldn't account for anyway. The man, the little girl, it was like trying to hug water; you just come away with an armful of nothing.

She did have something from that other life, though: an address book. It was still sticking out of her back pocket after she was pounded downhill through the miles of white, pressing heavy on her achy hip when she found herself on her knees in the shallows. May handled it like it was some precious alluvial deposit except the names inside meant nothing to her, as if written in a language she didn't understand.

Some nights Gruff went to his meeting in Hamburg. That's what he called it, his meeting. The state had taken away his license, so he thumbed rides there or Palmer drove him on occasion out of the goodness of his heart, and he talked about the bottle with a number of other people at the church. Gruff didn't hardly mention the meetings with her. He'd come back to the shack with the shine dulled in his eyes, smelling of cigarette smoke.

One night in late summer after they'd found a thin vein at Lucky Boy that afternoon, he told May about gold. A fire cracked in the oil drum across the yard and she could hear the propane lamp gasping inside.

His voice snagged in his throat, the scratchiness of an old record. "Gold—it's not just a mineral, it's a meaning," he explained to her. The fire spat out sparks. "Always has been. The Egyptians, the Greeks, the Romans—gold always meant the same thing, didn't need no translation. It goes back forever, lifetimes way before ours."

May considered her address book, how the names inside reached back to a life before this one, and understood what he said.

"You take away the 'l' and it's God." She could see moonlight gleaming in his eyes. "That means it's all tied together. The earth, the trees, the wind, the river—they can tell you things."

"I know," she said, remembering how the river called her name before it was May.

They listened to Horse Creek falling over rocks. "You listen to the trees and wind and river, and if you listen hard enough, you can tell where the gold is." Gruff scratched a spent match back and forth against his leg. "That and a good map," he laughed.

AS WAS HER HABIT, May scouted the cars and their license plates occupying the campsites at Goldfield on her walk back from the Jubilee. It was early November, a year and a half since the chain letter came, since that last night with Gruff.

There weren't but two cars tonight because of the lateness of the season. Only the hearty or bear hunters came this close to winter. Both cars had California plates.

During the spring and summer, that had been a different story. Come weekend, the six other campsites would fill with families or couples or solitary campers, the cars and trailers carrying plates from all over the U.S., some with the towns right there in raised lettering on the plates, towns and counties she'd never heard of before. The people were friendly, eager to find out about these hills, the hiking trails, the good fishing spots, eager also to share with her where they hailed from.

One summer night she talked to a family from Plano, Texas. "We got the best high-school football team in the state," the little boy said, "probably the country," his accent stretching the words as if it were a bungee cord.

May spent a good while by their fire and heard about their boating out on Lake Lavon, how god-awful hot the summers got. They invited her to sit down with them at the picnic table to eat dinner but she politely declined.

"I was wondering if you could do me a favor once you get back to Plano."

The family looked at her with puzzlement, the boy, his head cocked over a bit to the side the way a dog does when given a command it doesn't understand.

"I was hoping you'd mail this letter for me. I like having my letters go out with postmarks from all over."

Their faces relaxed again around the campfire and they assured her they would, sitting a bit prouder now that Plano would be part of her life. They talked more about Boulder Creek and she told them of a nice rill by the bridge beyond the campground, wide enough for fly casting, and May pulled the letter from her back pocket to give them before leaving.

The letter was going to Frakes, Kentucky, sent to a name she didn't know from the address book. This was the way she sent out all twenty letters during the spring and summer. She randomly picked a name from the book, addressed the letter in her blocky writing, and in would go the chain letter, she waiting to meet the people around the campfire in the evenings, looking for the license plates that sounded far off. Plano, Texas; Bossier City, Louisiana; Kingston, New York; Reston, Virginia; San Diego, California;

North Platte, Nebraska; Keane, New Hampshire—twenty of them in all.

But now, early November, there were just the two cars with the California plates, the both parked in adjacent sites, campers huddled around the fire ring. She was stiff from working with only the hand tools in the drift and she swung her arms around like waterwheels to loosen up the sockets, shaking out her day's work in the Jubilee. The people looked up when they heard her come by but she didn't stop; her twenty letters had gone out, all the links were connected, the chain cast out. On the way back to her camp-site she listened to the trees and wind and the river, listened for the gold.

Boulder Creek was running heavier now, the rains coming up high in the mountains, the trees moving more in the wind, freed from their burden of leaves. She listened and thought she heard something familiar but couldn't say, not exactly, what that was.

WHEN GRUFF FELL OFF the wagon a year and a half before, it was with a tremendous clatter. Everything was fine through close-out of Lucky Boy. After that, he turned darker with the season.

Gruff and May worked some small construction jobs, clearing and burning brush if weather permitted, to keep busy until spring and stocked in food. But in the Klamath the people mostly hunkered down for the duration like the black bears did or migrated somewhere else like warblers.

The snow piled up around Gruff's shack, the world closing in around them. Everything stopped; if Horse Creek didn't move the way it did, it would have frozen up and stopped, too. May could see Gruff wanted to keep himself moving. At first, he tried going to more meetings in Hamburg, but the traffic wasn't what it was during the summer on 96, and even in the summer it was only a trickle, so thumbing was next to impossible. Also he didn't feel quite right asking Palmer for a lift, no matter how good a Christian Palmer was, because they wouldn't be working together again until spring.

It was boredom that finally got him and strung him up. And Gruff and May eventually stopped talking the way they did out on the planks during the summer nights.

Gruff took to walking—to his meetings, to the store for any such thing, to the VFW hall to see if any jobs were posted, installing a woodstove, cutting wood, what have you, walking to just about anywhere his legs would carry him. His beard grew out and he looked even more like a bear, a restless one that'd been woken up early from a winter's sleep.

Just before the thaw in March, he got in his cups again, going on a three-day binge at the cabin, boozing on grain alcohol. He was a sloppy drunk at first, not mean, pissing himself, burbling the liquor out of him the way a baby spits up.

On the second day of the binge, he talked to May about gold again. "I know where the gold is." His voice was rougher yet from drink.

"A few more weeks we'll be working with Palmer and Murph again," she said, thinking that was what he was talking about, hoping this ugliness would pass with the season.

He swatted his hand a couple of times at that notion and some of the liquor came back up and out onto his shirt and he cursed to himself. "No, no. Not Lucky Boy. The *gold*," he said, his pupils narrowing in the red that surrounded them. He got up and fell, tried again and fell again, stumbled on rubber legs to the wall, and pried away one of the pine boards. He brought back a sheaf of papers.

"Gold," he said, thumping the papers with his thick hand.

She thought it was what Murph and Palmer looked at. Maps.

Gruff made a sound with his mouth, an exhaling full of derision. "This here's real gold, girlie."

And she came around to look.

"It's from the old Liberty Mine Company," he said. "They worked all over these parts until the War. Then the boys went off to Europe and the Pacific. They was digging trenches instead of drifts." He started waving his arms, wanting to say more, but the drink overtook him and all he could manage to do was put the old maps back and make his way to his bunk before spilling some more of his liquor out his mouth and falling asleep.

On the third day of the binge, Gruff mostly slept, waking up to sip some more, then knock out again. The following day he cleared, but he wasn't the same after. From then on, he looked at May with suspicion, unsure whether he'd shared with her his secret or not, not remembering. It grew worse. He'd come home from one of his walks and look like he was ready to shoot her, sizing her up with squinty eyes that threw off heat like fire.

The next week he got to tippling again and, coming back from a walk, lousy drunk, he started to accuse her of stealing his gold but his tongue was too thick, the words strangled in his mouth, and all he could make was animal sounds and he swatted her around the shack like she was no more than cloth and stuffing. When his arms grew punch heavy, he fell back onto the bunk, missed it, and thudded to the floor.

And May looked like she did the day she walked out of the river. After he collapsed she wrapped herself in blankets and didn't return for the whole night. It hurt to walk, but going back inside would only hurt more and so she walked. Horse Creek was running like an unbroken roan, brown and over its banks, the waters surging in the shadow of spring. She heard the sucking sounds, the yelling of the water again. But this time, seeing the fall line of the river, she knew it was Gruff being swept away and she didn't want to be carried with him.

She returned to the shack in the morning, opening the door more than timidly. His face was creased but he was sober and when he saw what he had done to her, the bruises and welts and cuts, his expression nearly folded in on itself. And again like the night before his words were strangled, but this time it was from shame, not drink.

"Go to a meeting," she said gently.

Gruff nodded and picked himself up.

"Please," May said through her swollen lips, "go to one of your meetings." And he did.

While Gruff was at his meeting in Hamburg, the mail came and in the delivery was the chain letter. Reading it the best she could, she felt the words run through her like electrical current. It told of a man in New Hampshire who didn't believe in the power of the words and his two daughters died. Another man in Illinois, however, had followed the directions of the letter, sending out copies anonymously to twenty people, and a wonderful fortune befell him.

May must have read the letter upwards of twenty times when Gruff was at his meeting, each time the picture the words made coming in clearer. Finally, she saw what she had to do and she folded the letter, gathered up her address book, went to the pine board, and pried the board away. The maps were still there and she took one of them, leaving the rest of the sheaf, thinking Gruff wouldn't miss the one, thinking this was what the letter meant. And then she quit the shack for good.

Just as she did when she came out of the river, May went south. The three things she brought with her—the address book, the letter, the map—were bound together in a magic knot, a golden chain.

And as May went south, down 3, the season changed and she left the Klamath, crossed the Siskiyous, and came into the forests of the northern Trinity Alps.

IN THE LIGHT OF the electric lantern hanging in May's tent at Goldfield, the stretched blue nylon ceiling was a curving phony sky in the cold November night. The campers at the adjacent campsites had settled down for the evening, their fires consuming themselves, and May couldn't see the flames anymore from the screen in her tent, not that she was looking much.

What May was studying was the map of the Jubilee. There were a lot of surveyor symbols and language she didn't understand, even more geological words with callouts. It didn't matter to her that she didn't know these words she couldn't hardly get her mouth around. It proved what Gruff had told her the summer they worked Lucky Boy. "Gold has meaning," she said in the tent now, knowing it was something greater than she could fully understand.

Despite all this ignorance, she knew where she was on the map, could trace her progress inside the adit and down the cross-cut. And that was enough for her. The old paper crinkled in her hands like folding money. The blue ink had turned in age to purple and brown.

Without fail, May looked at the map every night, her faith unshakable one night it would tell her more. "The letters have been sent," she said, saying what she had been saying nightly ever since handing the last of them to the little boy from Plano.

And after the map said nothing to her this night, she folded it up, switched off the light. May listened again, was always listening. The wind in the trees, the fast water in Boulder Creek running below the knob her tent was perched on—they told her the rains were coming soon.

AFTER QUITTING GRUFF AND before setting up camp at Goldfield, May worked at Wyntoon. The day she left him and thumbed south to the forests of the northern Trinity Alps, she saw a HELP WANTED sign at a gas station outside Trinity Center.

It was on the property of the Wyntoon Resort. With the spring and summer season coming, Wyntoon needed extra hands and May stayed on, working in the scullery at the restaurant, cleaning cabins, patching leaky canoes; whatever they would have her do, she did.

As payment, the owners gave her room and board and minimum wage, the room a small shack out by a stand of pines near the road. And that was enough—better, actually, than bunking with Gruff.

She kept to herself and she worked hard, nearly every day, although the work was much less taxing than working the hoists at Lucky Boy. And even if the owners thought she was an idiot, that was all right by her, too. It meant they left her alone.

Anyway, there were plenty enough things filling her head. The bruises and cuts and welts from Gruff healed in time, but she would wake from sleep in the dim light of the shack, bolt upright from dreaming he was pummeling her again. Sometimes she got the dream mixed up, saw the rapids in his eyes.

Other times the man and the little girl visited her. It was around this time that she got it inside her head that they were her husband and daughter, except she didn't feel any wifely or mother love for them and at the same time she considered they might be a trick.

It had been a year since she'd been delivered from the river, a year since this life began. May was one year old.

As time passed, the dreams of Gruff stopped and May missed him. This wasn't wifely love either. She liked the magic way he talked about gold during that summer before he fell off the wagon; she thought he understood what the river could tell a person. And to fill up some of the spaces inside her, she talked to him.

During the summer she caught a ride back to Coffee Creek, then walked the five miles up Coffee Creek Road to where the forest service trail was and hiked the mile to the Jubilee. She had been thinking about the address book, the chain letter, and the map in her shack and knew it was getting to be time.

Boulder Creek ran thin as it banded the trail. The trees stood stock-still in the heat, no wind to speak of. And May knew she would have to come back in the spring, when the river would be fat and muddy and the trees busy with blowing out winter, when they could tell her more. She stayed at Wyntoon through winter with the skeleton crew and left with the spring.

WHEN SHE AWOKE AT Goldfield her tent was hot with morning light despite the November chill, the two cars of the campers already gone. It was a handsome day, the purple underbellies of clouds sticking close to the higher elevations, the sun still strong even though it had already begun its sidewinder bend in the sky.

On the way to the Jubilee she watched Boulder Creek the way she always did. It was up a few inches, probably rained the night before higher up. And the wind confirmed this, carrying on it the damp and cold.

Inside the drift she fell into the comfortable rhythm of swinging, smoothing the face, swinging. She thought she saw a glimmer but it was flakes of quartz and she kept at it, the pickax marking time. "That was quartz, Gruff, not gold. But it's in here, the gold. They wouldn't have a map if there wasn't."

When her stomach started a conversation with her, May stopped for lunch, exiting the adit to eat by Boulder Creek. It was up yet another inch since this morning.

Settling back in the dark after she ate, her lantern making a little room of light in the void, she continued, her shoulders rolling with each throw of the pickax, her wrists flicking. She was getting close, she told herself between swings. "Just you wait, Gruff," she said to the darkness, "that gold's going to rise like a varicose vein."

And the darkness said back to her, "You thought you could fool me," in a voice full of rasps and nails.

At first May thought it was her head that was doing the talking and so she said, "I'm about to discover the meaning of gold, Gruff."

Out from the black, from further down the drift, he stepped, Gruff, big and terrible. "You're about to discover something else."

He stepped forward and May backed up. She didn't know if this was still her head, a trick or something, until he pushed her, and when her head bounced off the wall, her teeth bit tongue, tasted the salt of blood in her mouth—then she knew he was flesh.

May rolled back to the wall, using it to help her regain her footing.

Gruff said, "It's best to mind that jackleg, girlie," and he laughed, more a deep rumble than anything else. "I was thinking you might have left for good and maybe I lost my map. But I knew better."

He pushed her again and again her head snapped back into hard rock. She struck with her pickax and this time she hit vein, not gold, the carotid artery in his neck. He fell back, the blood spurting a good foot outward, and he made a horrible glugging noise from deep inside. He was grabbing frantically, pawing the air like an animal. May could smell that he'd evacuated his bladder and bowels as he shook there.

Then she heard it. From deep inside the adit came the sound of the trees and wind and river: the chittering of Gruff's limbs, the air rushing out of him in gusts, the washing of his blood onto waste rock. And what she heard dissolved the gold, the letter, the links that bound them together.

The tremors slowed, then stillness, another throb, then nothing. May looked at what was Gruff no more, an enormous body stinking of piss and shit and the smell of death already. And she left, Gruff, her pickax, her wheelbarrow, the hand tools, she left all of it. She kept moving on the forest service trail, the sound of the rising river in her ears as she ran. And she saw that this is the way it would be, so much of her life happening in the dark, the river washing it away. And she kept moving.

Between Knowing and Dying

I'M LOSING MY SELF like an old skin. Every day in the shower there's more of me, collecting in the drain, sloughing off, the snake I was. When I step out of the tub and shake, there I am, a little less of before, more of what I'm becoming.

I'm thirty-eight years old, thirty-eight and a half to be exact. There's no time to waste; we've done that plenty.

Here's the plan: We've run away, out of town and into the woods. It's magic, miles inside wilderness, an in-holding property is what they call it, five acres, our own canyon rim to rim, more trees than you can imagine. They come right up to the door, the trees. Ponderosas, madrones, dogwoods, pines, oaks. When the leaves fall, it sounds like big flakes of snow.

Wink says to me, "You can see why they call it ponderosa." She points way up, two hundred feet, high above where the bats fly. "Ponderous," she says. And it's a true thing, how the boughs droop.

I say, "I'm going to count all these trees. Just wait. You'll see."

Wink says, "Sure, sure," knowing how I lie. She's beautiful, Wink is.

Already I've made it up to the wilderness marker, one thousand three hundred thirty-nine trees.

Through the woods lives Alice. She's eighty-seven, has hiked every trail in these mountains, hiked clear through both her knees, hikes yet on a new set made from plastic and polymers. We see her on our walks, the day early, sun still not over the treetops.

"Madrones," she'll say. "Rare in these parts." The dogs circle like she's sheep. We nod, Wink and me, look at each other, consider how lucky we are, try to convince ourselves of it, even after what's happened.

Alice, she knows every last plant in the county, has written a book about them. We study it the way some people read the Bible, settle arguments with it: "Told you. That's a moon orchid. See?" We rush for it after every walk, pour over the color plates, our mouths wide open, as if children, as if the blooms will deflate, curl into nothing before we can name them.

"All these leaves," she'll say when we see her. "It's fuel. Have to rake them to keep the fire hazard down, you know."

Alice's husband, Horace, was the district ranger, used to have huge burn piles, we're told, just huge. "Hot as the sun" is how the ranchers down the road tell it.

Horace has been dead years. It's just Alice in the cabin. Before he died, he routed a sign for her. ALICE'S WONDERLAND, it says, a pine tree on either side; it hangs over the trail leading to her cabin.

"The leaves," I'll promise her. "I'll take care of it," I'll say. That and the dirt trail that climbs to Alice's and our cabin. There are erosion bumps cut into the hill, culverts under the ground, veins and arteries. I need to go at all of it with a pickax before the rains, before they clog up and the trail washes away.

But it's just Indian summer now. The days start slow, blue and white in the morning, cold, finally warming to a yellow firefly glow by afternoon. We walk the mornings, wave at Alice on her porch. I call to her across the meadow that Horace cleared in front of her cabin. "The leaves and the culvert!" I say. "I'm getting to it!"

I BURIED MY FATHER a month ago. We found out in April. He barely made September. Wink and I were in Alaska when we first heard the news, his disease. We didn't know about our new life then, maybe only a little, maybe only the edges, maybe only that last thought that sleep whispers in your ear come morning.

After we found out, we drove fast as hell in the Alaskan beater we'd rented, flying over frost heaves, perhaps trying to die ourselves, aspens straight and thin as pipe cleaners clicking by the window. Nights we stopped in towns at the foot of Denali, a spit in Kachemak Bay, a shank of the Matanuska glacier, Talkeetna, Homer, Tok, Northway. We drank tequila in roadhouses, traded stories with mountain climbers from Europe, natives from the Interior, dog sledders, professional drinkers, hunters. One night we sang "Moon River" to a friend in the lower forty-eight. The telephone was in the ladies' bathroom, a ten-foot grizzly under glass outside, keeping guard over the bar. The grizz was already rolled away for the night—twelve o'clock straight up, April sky still blue and going to royal. "Better be a quick song," the manager had said, hearing the racket, pushing a mop outside the bathroom, not as amused as we were. We made it as far as "huckleberry friend." Then one by one our faces broke, Wink, me, Libby, the woman we were traveling with, a friend who ate up adventure like it was pie, a hero of Wink's. Libby'd run every river in the state and was now going back for seconds.

We laughed for five minutes, forgot about my father completely.

"Get out of here," Wink said. "I have to pee."

"Hot damn," Libby said when she came out. "That's the farthest I've made it yet. 'Huckleberry friend.' A record."

MY FATHER HAD SAID to me in the five months between knowing and dying, "Get on with your life. I know you love me." He'd said, "Don't remember me like this. Just don't."

What I'll remember is he died the year Mickey Mantle went, that he looked like Joe DiMaggio except taller, that he had a disease named after Lou Gehrig. He died, improbably enough, the day after Ripken broke Gehrig's string of consecutive games. The truth.

What this pantheon of Yankees has to do with my father I can't say. We went to a game only once when I was a kid. That was it. The Yanks stunk up the place, the way they did. I remember my father backed his car into another man's in the parking lot after the game. "That's going to cost you, bub," the guy had said. I think he would have hit my father if I wasn't there. I remember my father, red-faced in that Bronx night. I wanted to protect him. I wanted to say, "Nobody talks to my pop like that."

WE'VE RUN AWAY TO the woods, Wink and me, fled the life we used to have. We drive slow now, no longer trying to die.

I can smell the rains these days. Pretty soon the fronts will come down from Alaska as if on tracks, one after the other, rain big as elephant tears. I imagine them sweeping down from the Brooks Range, blowing us the air we breathed six months ago, the first days of knowing.

Wink and I are burning leaves and duff, raking the fuel into small piles throughout our canyon, dogs playing tag all the while.

My father used to say to me, "I don't know what it is about this nature thing." He'd shake his head, laugh. "Just leaves me cold." I wish he was here with me now, right now. I'd say, "Dad, maybe all you need is a better jacket."

Alice comes along, hitching up the trail on her new knees. The dogs, Maggie and Kody, the little one, bring pinecones for her to throw, but she'll have none of it.

"Look," I say, "the leaves." The piles smoke in the fall air. There's already a moon the color of filmy teeth hanging in the sky.

She says, "Now, what about those erosion bumps, the culverts?" And she smiles, big and round, smiling for old Horace; she has to be, she's smiling so much.

She pulls her coat around her. Her grandson Cedric's in town, she tells us. Works for the forest service.

"Chip off the old block," I say. "Like Horace."

She waves away the thought, never considering any of my nonsense. "He's at the Forest Deli now," she says, "watching the game. On the dish. Yankees, I think. The playoffs."

I think of the Yankees, fallen leaves, my father in pinstripes, not Yankee, but the suit he was buried in, the last moments I had with him before he became fire and air. Horace comes to mind, too, that old ranger. Then I see Alice again. Alice, dusky as silver plate, somewhere miles and miles past her last legs, still plodding, though. Then I see this new life of ours, green, fresh, all the days, how much we have left.

I want to count each day, like my trees, like a record.

I want to dance Alice around the burning piles as long as her new pegs hold up. I want to sing "Moon River" again, see this time if we can make it all the way past "huckleberry friend."

Instead I say, "The culverts and bumps. Next on my list. Promise."

Alice smiles, smaller this time.

Sure as we're standing there, sure as that, I decide we're going to live forever.

It's Me Again

THERE HAVE GOT TO be a thousand and one memories camping with me in this tent: one of those canvas army surplus jobs, its green the color of pine needles; an unmistakable nosegay of mildew and mothballs. Just one whiff—that's all it takes for the smell to fly from my potato nose to that hodgepodge where my memories are stored away.

What I remember is a trip to King's Canyon with my first wife and only son, he not eight at the time, the boy sitting in the circle of my arms and legs, the two of us watching the blue night on a hard-rock ledge outside this tent, the stars falling soft as pearls through water.

"Look," I whispered into the dish of his ear. "Orion. The hunter." And the wordless sound he made was wonder, a puff blown through little lips. "Someday," I said. "The two of us. Hunting."

He hugged me close, just my little man and me out there, the wife in the tent, asleep. "Dad," he said, his soft voice. "Dad."

"I know," I said. "It'll be great. You and me. Promise."

That's not all. Inside every memory is another. What I remember deep inside this one is an overnight when I was no more than my son's age then, the same mantle of night sky, cicadas buzzing like high-voltage lines, my friends and me shooting at the Illinois night with slingshots. It was a raccoon that Dickie Most nailed outside the circle of campfire light, a mama. We watched it die, its stomach fat with babies, rising, then not, all of us hopped up later from the kill, crazy boys, up all night.

There's something deeper yet. I imagine a million Boy Scouts in this tent before me, each scout making a tent within this one, their newly hardened desire propping up cotton-batting sleeping bags like stakes.

And following the course of these memories inside memories I know now this is our place. Men outside in the dark.

It's two hundred yards to the house where my new wife, Audrey, is now. There's a light going in her bedroom, the rest of the house black. It might as well be a thousand miles, the way things are.

Tonight it's quiet in the rest of the cabins, the summer rush come and gone. Four guests only. An old couple who've come up to the Trinities for twenty-five years now, the kind of story that's an advertisement for marriage. A blocky woman traveling alone with her ancient shepherd mix, Atlas. A fisherman with rummy eyes.

Except for hellos I don't know any of them. Still they're more welcome here than me, ever since my exile to this fusty tent pitched in the meadow. I know from last year's fall, my first in the Trinities, how frosty October nights are. Audrey has nothing on them.

I scooch down in the bag, pull it around, leave the tent fly open. You can hear Ripple Creek these days. The wind spins though the valley now, running as if on a wire between Billy's Peak and Bonanza King, and I think of all the things I miss.

Audrey, certainly.

My son, too. It's more than six years since that camping trip to King's Canyon, back when he was still Frank Jr.

These days, I don't know who he is. He seems to have a better handle on it than me. "Call me Spider," he'd said a little over a year ago. And I did.

Later, after Audrey and Ramona came into our lives, he said, "I'm Colt," and Colt it was.

Me, I have a whole different name for it. Puberty. I feel for the kid. His face is so broken out, the pimples look like a connect-the-dots for an abstract painting. The bottom's dropped out of his cute little tenor, too, his voice now sounding like someone's stepping on a frog. And, of course, there's testosterone coming out all over like a shook-up bottle of beer.

I love the boy so much it hurts, haven't seen him since we were booted out last Friday. He's roaming over this countryside with his gun, I think, foraging among the pines and dogwoods and cedars, an animal. The kid's in my prayers, whatever his name is.

I miss Ramona, my stepdaughter. Poor zombie girl with her Lyme disease. It's like God decided puberty's not enough for this one; let's raise the ante. She's riding out the tremors and swollen joints over in cabin 4, the little one near the woods where Ripple Creek funnels into the East Fork. I peeked in her window earlier, my nightly rounds, but didn't see her.

And, of course, I miss knitting. In the old days before the kid and I moved from Weaverville, I'd wrap the evenings in yarn and stitchery. It was a marvelous way to shave down lonely hours. A swallow of scotch next to my elbow. My plaid La-Z-Boy tilted back in cruise control, head- and footrests fully extended; I miss that chair also, the Big Easy.

Audrey didn't like the knitting, said it wasn't seemly for a man to do. "Crikey," I said. "Rosey Grier knits," I told her. But the fact of a three-hundred-pound Hall of Fame lineman never really carried any weight with her.

So here I am. Alone. In this tent. Nothing to do with my hands. The temperature diving. The stars vibrating like crazy in the night sky. The wind in the trees. My boy, only God knows where.

There is one bright spot. My new toupee. It not only lops years off my appearance and gives me the kind of luxuriant hair that women go for, it's keeping me warm these chilly nights. You lose seventy-five percent of your body heat through the top of your head. Without the rug, I'd be congealed. It's not much comfort, I admit. I take what I can get these days.

It didn't always used to be this way.

After wife number one ran out on us, the boy and I moved north, climbed the state like steps all the way to Weaverville. It's a lovely little frontier town, a handful of streets that all run into Main, not a fax machine or traffic light in the whole of the place, a good many of the townspeople still relying on woodstoves for heating and cooking.

When the night wind blows into Weaverville, it comes from somewhere I've never been, blows straight through the gap between Weaver Bally and Oregon Mountain, smells of trees and water and earth. What you feel then is something wild running inside you. And you throw another log on the fire, look out the window into a sky with more stars than you've ever seen before, feel the forest that's right outside the door pressing in on you like people in a crowded elevator. And you wait for the wood to take. And when it does, you truly understand what the word *home* means.

I thought we could build a new future in Weaverville but the soil proved too rocky. Some bad business with a convenience store. It's old news now, best not to even go into it. What I will say is those were dark days last winter, the boy running wild, barely talking. We had to get out.

I wasn't working, the both of us living off savings, any prospect buried under a wall of snow. I knitted the days away—two king-sized afghans, a sweater, scarf, ski cap, one half of a mitten pair. Then the season broke.

That was just about the time I saw the ad in the *Trinity Journal*. It was in the back, the classifieds, a skinny listing in agate. *Single woman*, the ad said; *companionship*, it said; and *teenage daughter*.

I figured what the hey, called the number. Audrey. She had a delightful voice, like a bird, used to be a singer in a bar band, she told me.

"Coffee Creek," she said on the phone. "That's where I live."

"Sounds wonderful," I said.

"Oh, so you know it."

I laughed. "I know coffee," I said and she laughed, too, and it was a beautiful thing, it was, loose as rocks rolling down a hillside. "I'm new to the area, to tell you the truth," I said. "Actually, I'm not new. I'm forty."

"Perfect," she said.

We talked and it was easy and the recent sorry months seemed like a washed-out memory. Near the end of the conversation she said, "Do you want to come up here? For a date I mean."

"I'd love to."

"Saturday, Frank?"

"Saturday it is," I said.

"I own a little resort up here," she said. "Cabins, really."

I paused. "I'm between things," I said. "Waiting for the right opportunity."

"Can I be Frank with you?" she said. We both had a good chuckle at that. She said, "Frank, you sound like the kind of man who knows when it comes along. Opportunity."

"Saturday," I said.

"Exactly," she said.

AFTER WE HUNG UP I looked on the map for Coffee Creek. It was way up on the north shore of Trinity Lake, a crossroads. After all these months of being snowbound, the picture I had in my mind was green and romantic and alive.

"I'll be gone all day today," I said to the kid Saturday morning. "Coffee Creek," I said.

"Whatever," he said. He'd stopped making eye contact with me a while ago, his eyes always locked on the wall behind me.

There are times when you want to hug your kid tight, tell him the night isn't so dark. This was one of those times. But I did nothing. We were men; we circled each other like timberwolves. I tried to bisect the circle anyway. "It's a date," I said. "In Coffee Creek."

"Sure, Big F," he said and shoveled Froot Loops into his mouth, slurped the pink-stained milk in his bowl, got up, left the kitchen.

The ride was glorious, the Civic humming along like a kazoo. After the flats and the dump, Trinity Lakes Boulevard turned into 3, and once clear of town, the Alps lined up in my lefthand window, snowcapped. Upside-down white beards is how it looked.

And 3 was mine. Only five other vehicles in the whole forty-five-mile trip. So many different greens all around me, spring rooting everywhere, the forest coming all the way up to the edge of the road.

And then the lake. Some blue at first between the trees, then the whole of it spreading like a picnic blanket before me. And then I was there.

The sign on Eagle Creek Loop read CREEKSIDE CABINS and behind the split-rail fence were a number of peely cottages, a falling barn, overgrown meadow, the driveway weedy and rutted.

And Audrey, who was lovely.

From our phone conversation, I didn't quite know what to expect but she was better than anything I'd conjured. She had the big and solid classic lines of a '57 Chevy. Hair that was crow black. Eyes that weren't so much blue as sky. A big, goofy smile, teeth as perfect as piano keys.

"You must be Frank," she said.

"Always," I said and she let go of the horse trailer she was fiddling with, laughed that laugh, slapping her hand against jeans stretched tight across her thigh.

"Always," she said, "that kills me," her voice like a song. She looked down at the tongue to the trailer, picked it back up from where she'd dropped it. "How does horseback riding grab you? Stoddard Lake," she said. "Should be amazing. Just us."

"Sounds great," I said.

"Great," she said, "great." She let the tongue go again, slipped her arm through mine, pulled me along the driveway. "Let's go meet Ramona." Along the way Audrey stopped, looked me square. "There's something you should know," she said and told me about the girl's Lyme disease. "It's okay," she said. "We're managing. Barely."

It wasn't a house they were living in but one of the cabins. There weren't any guests in any of the other ones as far as I could see, and if their cabin was any indication, I knew why. The pine paneling was pulling away from the wall, the kitchen counter stained a dark berry color, a smell inside as rank as old brussels sprouts.

Ramona was vampire white with orange hair that had to have been dyed. She looked ready to pick a fight with me the minute I came through the door, only didn't seem to have enough energy to back it up.

"Why don't you two talk," Audrey said, "while I load Harry and DeSoto in the trailer."

After Audrey left, the girl and I looked at each other for a while. "So," she said finally. "You're the one." She fixed right on me, her dead green eyes.

"The one what?" I said.

The girl had a dull smirk, squinted her eyes, face rumpled as a bedsheet.

I said, "I have a boy who I bet is your age," and pulled out my wallet, showed the picture, the one back when he had the do where his hair was shaved off on both sides but long and black and greasy on top. "Maybe you know him from school."

She exhaled, a long draggy wind, looked like she'd fall asleep on me right there.

I saw Audrey through the window leading the horses out of the barn. Up on the bookshelf in the living room was one of those Russian dolls, the kind where each nests inside another and another and so on. "I love these things," I said, picking it up. "It's like a secret. Or a surprise. You always want to get to the bottom."

"Don't touch that," she said, life coming into her for the first time. She walked over, took it from my hands, her nails long and painted red. "That's from Freddie," she said.

"Sorry." I tried to smooth things over. "That Lyme disease thing. Must be tough. My heart goes out to you. Really."

"Tell me about it," she said.

Audrey came back into the cabin at this point. "You two fast friends yet?" she said. Then to me, "We're about ready to go, Frank." She went over to the girl, gave her a big hug, ran her fingers through her orange hair like a comb. "Have a good day, Monie," she said. "Remember what the doctor said. A little walk wouldn't hurt."

We bumped along the ten-mile forest service road to the trail-head in her rusty Dodge pickup, pulling the horses.

It was slow going. Along the way she told me her story. Her husband, Freddie, was a bounder through and through. They used to be in the band together; he was the guitarist. They'd put a little money away, bought the cabins. But his heart wasn't ever in it. "The last straw," she said. "Found him screwing some little tail right here. In cabin four. Asshole couldn't even rent a motel."

Lyme disease was another low card. She said the whole health insurance thing was a jumble, said it ate up all the money that should have been going for upkeep.

When she was done, her eyes were shiny marbles. I felt my own heart tightening, thought I should say something and told her my story, the whole nasty bit, Weaverville, Elise, how the boy after she left flew from me like a hunted animal. Once I was done, she pulled the emergency brake, tugged me to her, the stick shift digging in my leg. "We're two of a kind, aren't we?" she said.

After she parked the Dodge, Audrey showed me how to mount DeSoto. We clopped along, watching spring jump up through the soil, the day warming to hot.

It had been so long since I'd talked to a woman. I felt kingly riding DeSoto, she bobbing, Audrey drinking in what I was saying.

"She likes you," Audrey said. "Ramona."

I thought of the tired girl back in the stinky cabin, my own boy in Weaverville, what a crusty seed he was—it seemed there were so many different ways for kids to be angry these days.

"I can tell," Audrey said. "She does."

The last mile she held my hand the whole way. I didn't think the day could get any more beautiful. But we rounded the corner, the blue and green manzanita shrubs gave way, and there in the bowl of the land at six thousand feet was Stoddard Lake, twenty-five acres of water smooth and clear as stretched plastic wrap, the pines and oaks growing right up to the nubby grass at lake's edge, a fat oak deadfall rising out of the shallows like the hull of an old clipper, warblers describing pinwheels, chasing one another in the thin air. I was practically gagging on the splendor of it all, nobody else within miles.

Audrey'd packed a lunch. We spread out a blanket, nibbled cheese and little sandwiches and fruit, talked about everything. When it seemed like we'd exhausted it all, the food, the conversation, I lay back and looked at the sky, listened to Harry and DeSoto snorting, thought to myself this is what happy is, Weaverville so far away. And then Audrey's face hovered over me, blocked out the white-blue sky. And she kissed me.

"This is going to sound crazy," she said. "No. Forget it."

"Go on," I said. "What?"

"This is going to sound crazy." She squeezed her eyes closed. "Will you marry me?" she said.

Then she did something else crazy. She took off all her clothes. It seemed my head was full of flies, couldn't work with the all the things being fed me.

She looked lovely. Her breasts were big as the water balloons we'd lobbed off the roof of our house when we were kids. I could go on but it wouldn't be right. Breasts are simply a miraculous invention of flesh and womanhood. Respect must be paid.

Anyway, before I could take all of her in, she ran into the lake, let out a scream that echoed, bouncing back and forth from trees to the rock face that climbed up to Billy's Peak.

I found I was peeling the clothes off me, too, and followed her, the water colder than anything I could imagine, sucking the breath and voice right out of me. We gripped each other, treaded water together, myself below curling up in the ice water like an old party favor.

I said, "I do," and gasped, completely out of my mind, the cold on the outside, fire within. "I mean," I said, "I will. Marry you."

Running a string of cabins is a wonderful job. So much splendid work: weeding, mowing, propping up the barn, scraping, painting, mending, scooping out the swimming hole. I had a list going long as my arm, and like my boy, it kept growing every time I turned around.

I fell for Coffee Creek about as hard as I did for Audrey. Two hundred independent souls living under the trees. No town to speak of. A general store. A café. If you want a stiff drink, you've got to drive eight winding miles to Trinity Center.

It's the kind of place where you can leave the shades up at night. The locals, they're a good lot, keep to themselves, so much space for everybody up here, they let you breathe.

The property at the cabins is sixteen magnificent acres, a wedge of heaven banded by Ripple Creek, the wider, faster Trinity East Fork, Harry and DeSoto's pasture, the woods.

With everything getting made over, the cabins, our lives, I figured it was time for me, too. I mailed away for the rug. It's an amazing thing. You clip off a few hairs, circle your type of baldness (mine's a big horseshoe shape) measure the area to be patched, fill in some information about allergies.

Three weeks later the UPS truck scooted up Eagle Creek with the genuine article. The boy thought I was nuts. Audrey squawked like a chicken. She was still having a hard time getting over my knitting. Ramona just looked at me with her lifeless eyes.

It was then I decided maybe I was pushing things too hard, giving my all to work, not having anything left for family. I can be that way; ask wife number one.

With Audrey, after the slam-bang marriage, things had settled into something a lot less giddy. The knitting, the toupee—she was laughing these days, only it wasn't the same as before. "So *this* is what's inside the package," she'd said, sounding more sharp than musical.

Back when I first told my boy about all my new plans, he looked away, shook his head, sucked on a tooth. "Son, it's going to be a lot more fun than Weaverville," I said. "Trust me."

For his birthday I recalled the promise I'd made in King's Canyon, hunting, that blue night on the ledge outside the tent now clouded, a dusty memory. I bought him a pump-action rifle hoping he'd remember, too. Maybe he did: I have to admit the kid seemed a lot less miserable than usual. "Sweet," he'd said, whistled low when I gave it to him. He started reading gun magazines, shaved all the hair off his head.

While I was busy working the cabins, I'd hear his blasts all day. He started coming home with shot-up little varmints. This was about the time of the second name change, from Spider to Colt, for the sidearm manufacturer.

In my heart, I hoped the two kids would get along, the four of us be one happy family. But even though they were two odd ducks, Colt and Ramona, they acted like they were from different flocks. Nights he'd hang dead squirrels and chipmunks outside her window. Ramona'd wake up screaming. Then Audrey would light into me, almost drying up the scalp adhesive that held the rug down on my head.

I HAD ONE MORE ace. What with all the work, the brochure, the advertising, Ramona's medications and treatment, my savings were getting thin. But I knew living in that little cabin wasn't a home. Down the road by the café was a beauty for sale: old fashioned, big kitchen, wide stairway that led up to a gabled second floor.

It was crazy. I cleared out the land near the barn. Then on a bright July morning, the truck came, hoisted the whole deal out of its foundation, crawled the four and a half miles to the cabins. I had to get a permit to close 3 for the afternoon. Practically the entire town turned out to watch the procession, the wideload moving at two miles per, me walking around the house the whole way like a little kid.

Ramona decided she'd stay in cabin 4 but I figured she'd come around. Later that night, the house set in place, I walked outside, stars blinking, ran my hand around all of it.

Home, I thought. Later I dreamt the feeling would last forever.

MAYBE IT WAS THE kids all along.

They were poison. Colt was always pulling pranks. Audrey had hooked up an intercom in Ramona's cabin and its buzzer was sounding in the new house all hours because of him.

By Labor Day the wife was in full retreat. We seemed so far from that afternoon of horseback riding at Stoddard Lake. I wanted to find our way back, knew it would be up to me to get us there.

I was swinging the scythe in the clumps of sumac near the kiddie swings one September Saturday, sweat running down my neck. I saw the kid trudging back from Horse Flat, gun in one hand, plugged varmint the other.

"Colt," I called, waved him over.

He came in a rolling walk, held up the animal.

"Good, son," I said. "Good." I looked at the bristles that were his hair, thought about asking him why he'd shaved it all off. "I used to be pretty good myself," I said. "ROTC."

He stared at me, mouth pursed like he wanted to spit a tooth.

"We need to talk," I said.

"Shoot," he said.

"Man to man," I said. "About your sister."

"She's not my sister."

"Stepsister, then." I looked at him and for a scary few moments I didn't know who the heck he was, couldn't see any of me in him. The words I'd rehearsed all day, about how we should all get along, what it would mean to me, spun in my head.

"What are you saying?" he said.

"Could you just go easy on her?" I said. "It would make things much better between me and your mother."

"She's not my mother."

I smiled. "Try giving Ramona a hug," I said. "All I ask. You'd be surprised."

The kid shrugged, started for the house, twirled the animal like it was a bola. I watched him, couldn't stop the thought of that funny, lovable kid I used to know, Frank Jr., the one who used to race me around the block in Loma Linda, the two of us chasing down the ice cream truck, his mother watching from the front window, him laughing to beat the band.

AFTER I CLEANED UP, I went over to Ramona's. "Knock, knock," I said at the screen door. Music was on. She'd just returned from her walk with Audrey. That was something the wife had been doing lately so the girl got some aerobic exercise.

"Who's there?" Ramona said.

"Me."

"Me who?" She came to the door, stood on the other side, slouching, more bored than any fifteen-year-old I'd ever seen.

"Don't know," I said. "No punch line."

"Then you can't come in." She turned, went back into the living room.

I opened the door anyway, followed her. "Just want to talk," I said. "Get so goshdarn busy I never get the chance." She locked on me with laser eyes, an uncomfortable thing; I'd grown so used to my shifty son. "You can be Frank with me," I said and laughed. "A little joke the boy and I used to have."

"Can I be?" she said. "Frank? That thing on your head looks like something died and landed there."

I said, "You know, I'm not your father."

"Duh."

"But," I said, "I am married to your mother. I want to make her happy."

She crinkled her nose, said, "How much money do you have left?"

I waved my hand. "We're getting a little far afield. I came to talk about Colt. About giving him a chance."

"Giving him a chance," she said.

"Right. I know you two could get along. If only you . . ." I saw the passive catheter in her arm, her amoxicillin drip. It stopped me.

"Give him a chance," she said.

"Exactly." I remembered my suggestion to the boy. "Try a hug," I said. "You'd be surprised."

"A hug." She looked at me, smiled as if she had a secret and wasn't going to tell. Whatever. It was a smile.

IT ALL CAME BACK to King's Canyon. Hunting.

The intercom buzzed just as I was serving the turkey brochettes I'd made for Audrey and the boy that night.

"Perfect," Audrey said, gave a tired laugh like the mower when it didn't turn over.

"It's probably nothing," I said, went to pat her, but she pulled away.

"I'm going out," Colt said, made for the door.

"No sir, mister," I said.

The three of us walked over, the nights cooler now, navy evenings where the bugs flew slow, easy game for the bats.

Ramona was out on the porch. "Look at this," she said, pointed at something red hanging on monofilament. The girl had on jeans and a little T. Except for all her white skin—she could have been Dracula's prom date—I noticed for the first time that Ramona was okay looking.

"What is this?" Audrey said, poked it with a stick.

"I don't know," I said and turned. "Colt?"

"A marten's heart," he said. "Indians used it to heal things." He looked Ramona straight in the eyes.

"Terrific," Audrey said. "I marry the father of Davy Crockett."

I pulled the boy aside, knocked down the heart, didn't want any guests to see. Audrey took Ramona into the cabin. I saw her setting up the IV through the window, trying to settle the girl.

"Listen, son," I said. "I know you meant well." We walked down by Ripple Creek. It was only a string of water these days. "It's that Ramona's sick," I said. "The medicine makes her jumpy. Women," I said.

The kid stared at the water.

I tried a different tack, my promise made over six years ago, a lifetime ago. "If you do this for me," I said, "I'll do something for you." Deer season opened in a week, in October. He was too young for a license but the two of us could go. "Deer hunting for a hug for Ramona. All I ask," I said. "The two of us. Hunting," I said. "It'll be great. You and me."

And the boy smiled at me, looked me in the eye, the first time in a coon's age. "Deer season," he said.

I swear for a moment I saw Frank Jr. again.

There's always someone watching.

Example. After Audrey and I got married. We'd taken the honeymoon room in the Lewiston Hotel for the night, the one with mirrors. We were in bed, doing what married people do. I looked in one of the mirrors, saw it reflected in the opposite mirror. And in that one I saw the other inside it yet again. On and on.

I began counting all the gorgeous breasts and, in a bolt, understood what this business was with mirrors and love. You can stand outside yourself, see from the outside. In that sea of bosoms, I couldn't stop. The last stage of my rocket fired. I fell back to earth.

What I think we really want is to see from the outside, I really do.

Another example. Our summer traffic slacked off after Labor Day, only a few guests since. There was a woman staying in cabin 2. One afternoon I was chopping wood when she walked by on the way to the swimming hole.

"I think I have a mouse," she said.

"No doubt. The woods," I said, smiled.

"There's a gap in the wall by the cabinet," she said. "I think it came from there. Ate my onion dip mix."

"I'll get on it." I went back to chopping. Later I remembered, grabbed a hammer, nails, plywood scrap, walked over. Cabin 2 faces Ripple Creek, is the most private.

She was on the lounge chair, top off, sunning herself, never heard me. Dazzling, it was. Breasts with *lift*. They were . . . the only word is *bulby*. Sheen of lotion on them. Actually bent and twisted the sunlight.

I was spellbound. The wife and I hadn't done anything since the hotel, weren't even sleeping in the same room, said I snored.

Looking at those breasts, I remembered a recent night. Audrey had shot out of her bedroom. I thought this was my chance. Her legs were jackhammering as if she were running the tire drill for the football team. I chased after her.

It turned out to be a mouse also.

Now, this woman's lovely, bulby breasts not twenty yards away, I wished I could freeze time into a snapshot. She spread more lotion. Maybe the river quieted, maybe I breathed. She sat up, held her hand to block the sun, looked my way.

"It's me again," I said. "The mouse." I showed the hammer. Her top went on in a flash. The afterimage is still burned on my retinae.

Maybe it all boils down to this.

There's something I liked to do. Nobody had the faintest. I worked on Ramona's cabin when she was out on her daily walk with Audrey—everybody knew that.

This is it: I came across some magazines in the closet behind a board, must have been Freddie's, dreadful names like *Booby Patch*. When the girl was out walking with her mother, I'd sneak into the closet, admire the marvelous feats of human engineering.

There was more. I liked to knit while doing it. It can settle a man. What with the wife and the warring kids, me bleeding money on the cabins, things had become tense. I didn't do anything else, mind you. Just me knitting and the magazines. Sweaters for the kids. An animal on each—bear for Ramona, cougar for Colt.

IT WAS THE OPENING day for deer season.

Things had quieted. I was feeling pretty good about the situation, I have to admit; my talk seemed to have worked. The boy, God bless him, had even been taking food over to Ramona, the special diet that Audrey prepared for her. Nights he'd slip out of his basement room, walking the hills I figured, too antsy to sleep with the thoughts of big game he'd soon have in his sights. And the wife, she wasn't letting me in her bedroom yet. But still, the door didn't seem completely shut.

The boy and I rose early, four A.M., shared a solemn breakfast, set out for the countryside. I had my best game face on but inside was all sugar excitement. This was what men did, what fathers and sons did—a tradition that went back forever. What it meant for the boy and me was a new beginning. We'd go into the wilderness, come out the other side. Amazing what killing an animal can do for you.

All week I had the picture of the day in my mind. We would talk, real heart-to-hearts, tell off-color jokes, slap backs, trade high fives. But in that cold, dark, dewy morning, I saw this wasn't to be.

Hunting was quiet, stealthy work. My boy, outfitted like a commando, his double barrel in hand, head on a slow, even swivel, treaded light as an angel. He shushed me whenever I started to talk. We walked together. And that was enough.

After three miles, we hunkered down in a wallow. It was beautiful, the pine smell, dogwood leaves falling, the cold, damp earth under us.

Lying in silent wait all those hours with the boy, I understood hunting, the seeing but not being seen. While he watched for game, I watched him—his pillow lips, Elise's lips, softness around the eyes, raised rash like chicken skin on the back of his neck.

Every so often he looked at me, no fight in those eyes. We didn't have to talk. I'd stalked the Frank Jr. eluding me the last two years, found him. And I knew precisely what to do when the moment of truth came, after the trigger squeezed and the deer fell. I'd hug him to me, say, "That's my boy. *That's my boy.*"

Right after three in the afternoon a buck ambled into the draw. Colt had big eyes. I didn't breathe, counted eight points. The kid pulled, the buck falling, the crack of the shot slapping me.

And then something strange happened. The boy got up, walked the fifty yards like a robot. I followed, ready to hug him and say what I'd planned. I neared him, saw his shoulders from behind, shaking, the kid sobbing, tears dripping on the ground.

And I did nothing. I stood there, a tree, did nothing.

His back to me, he over the animal, he finally said, "I miss her. Mom."

"Audrey?" I said, surprised.

"*Mom.*"

Then he field-dressed the deer. We dragged it out.

He said one thing on the way back: "She's playing you. The money."

I thought of the day at Stoddard Lake, was going to say, "You don't understand love, son," but didn't.

DINNER THAT NIGHT WAS hushed. The boy didn't even sit down with us, Audrey remote as ever.

Midway through the meal, the intercom gave out a long, steady buzz, the two of us falling out, our drill.

Ramona was on the porch, the boy kneeling on the ground in front.

"That's how I got it," she was yelling at the boy.

"Bullshit. None here," he said.

"*Colt*," she said.

When we got closer, I saw what he was kneeling over. The deer.

"Mom," Ramona said. "You believe this?" Audrey pulled the girl inside.

"Fuck you, Colt," Ramona called from the living room. "Fuck you."

"Fuck yourself," the boy said.

Audrey came to the screen door. "Deal with this," she said to me. "It's your son who's the tick." She went back to Ramona.

"Son, if you can't put your carcass away," I said, "you can't go hunting."

He stared at me, his eyes hurt, pinching at the corners, stood up, dragged off the deer, didn't come home that night.

THE NEXT DAY WAS taut. I worried about the boy, hadn't seen Ramona at all. Audrey didn't even stick around, set out early on a full-day ride on Harry.

Knitting was what I needed. Badly. When the time came for the kid's daily walk, I peeked in the cabin, saw she was gone. I hadn't heard Audrey return, but I'd been busy over in cabin 3, fixing a balky pilot light.

I stole into the closet. Everything was going great guns, the needles flying, most of the left arm for Ramona's sweater done, all those juddering magazine bosoms next to me.

And then I heard it, thought it was the wife and the girl returning. I didn't know what to do. I remembered yesterday's hunting, sat quiet, the closet door open a sliver.

It wasn't the wife. Ramona came in with the boy, the poison

twins. I was about to bust out, break up the inevitable fight. She lifted her hands. I thought she was about to hit him but they rested on his shoulders instead. She pulled him close, kissed him.

Then their clothes came off. And they went through movements as old as humankind. She was so white, the girl, had Colt come from behind, his hands leaving red marks on her rear, her sides. They moved in that rhythm. Fast, faster.

"Shoot," she said, voice dusky. "Shoot." The boy clenched, head back, the girl whinnying deep in her throat. They fell loose against the wall.

I had a tangle of emotions running inside. This was stepbrother, stepsister, their jiggering one tiny step above the animals. I felt something else, too, sitting on top of everything like a big cake decoration: *pride*. He was one of us, the company of men.

I was flushed, didn't realize what I was doing, must have leaned on the door. It gave way and I tumbled out, fell forward, the knitting still in my hands. "That's my boy!" I yelled. "That's my boy."

And at that moment Audrey came in the front door. Ramona and Colt, I saw, were pressed against the intercom. They never realized it.

The wife's mouth dropped, a trapdoor. She took it all in, the kids naked, dripping love, me on my knees.

I stood.

"*Knitting*," she said, came at me.

"Rosey Grier knits," I said.

She gave me one right across the nose. I flew into the bookcase. The Russian doll from Freddie tipped, fell, spilling the dolls inside, all of them clattering, rolling around the floor.

Even through watery eyes I saw the whole thing clearly, everything, what was inside the kids' aggression for each other all along, what was really inside this marriage. I understood.

The boy picked up his ball of clothes, lit out the door. That night I followed, the new house locked to me.

THIS TENT ISN'T SUCH a bad place.

There are times when I lie here, when the wind blows hard, a Siberian express. At those times, it's a dark night. I don't trust my thoughts, think of my tapped-out savings account, think of what I'll name this chapter of my life.

Other nights, though, when it's calm I can hear Harry nickering to DeSoto across the pasture, then DeSoto's hooves drumming as she nears. I consider the distance. I know a whole house can be picked up, replanted somewhere else.

And it's then that I think there must be something still inside all this. I think . . . I hope . . . There has to be.

Fish Story

WE WENT FISHING ONCE the settlement came from my thieving accountant. It wasn't a ton of money, just enough. Made us drunk at first, the money. We bought an old railroad flatcar to bridge the river, then an ancient caboose to live in, under the ponderosa. This is tree country, no tracks for hundreds of miles.

The forest service said we were nuts, about the flatcar, said a century flood would wash it out, carry it downriver, where maybe it'd kill somebody. "Besides," they said, "why'd anybody want to live in a caboose?"

Jess and me just laughed at those jokers, her eyes bluer than the Trinity sky, gleamers. She has killer eyes.

What all of them had to say, the forest service, insurance company—it didn't matter. We had the money. I haven't always done right by Jess, I'll admit that straight away. These days I'm trying, though. I have high hopes. She's a softy, besides, a forgiver, used to cry at soda pop commercials, the one with black labs.

Once the trains got trucked in, I manufactured a big wooden sign. It says CLOSED. I carved out others that say GO AWAY and I

HAVE A LAWYER AND I KNOW HOW TO USE HIM. I hung all three on trees, high up, at property's edge. There's an arrow now sunk deep in the lawyer one, an attorney-hating deer hunter, no doubt. Jess thinks maybe it's Cockeye Joe, the antique Wintu we share the hill with. "Too easy," I tell her. "An Indian shooting arrows at lawyers."

There's a rule in the Trinities this year regarding fishing, the size you can take out, nothing over twenty-two inches, a year with a bumper supply of fall-run chinooks yet. But still, no.

We think it's a riot, the law. We hold the riparian rights on our stretch of water, and, as a result, devise our own rules. We've out-lawed fly fishing, for example, entirely too fussy, all the jiggery pokery. The rigs we use are strictly swivels, spoons, spinners, no live bait, no pork rinds. Here's how it works: the fish get irritated by the sound, the subaural vibrations. Then they strike, pissed off to their very gills. It works like sorcery.

We fish naked, too, natives, me and Jess. She's thirty-six, still looks girlish in an exciting way, Jess working the rod, a metronome, wedge of private velvet below, above, breasts like lovely twin planets frozen in orbit.

It's a game, how we do it. I'll go until I land one, then Jess tries to better me, catch a bigger one, back and forth. She turns fierce-some, hard as granite, sharp. And I believe then it's not only about fishing, this contest. I figure if this is how we go at each other these days, seeing who can yank out the biggest fish, drowning them in a sea of air, that's okay.

Sometimes, say my line fouls on cast, she sneaks off, climbs a tree. She spies on me from up there, watches. I can see those mirror eyes in the green.

We've never established a limit on our section of river. I'll stop, but Jess, she'll continue to throw line until she catches every last

fish on the continent, maybe the world. Then we turn into fish ourselves, laze in the currents, the pools, speckled rocks. The water
must fall straight down from the polar cap, that cold. It's no matter
to Jess: she's flushed with victory. Even so, I get scared it's not
enough for her, the fish, never will be. She lies back, closes her
eyes. She looks as if she's counting back from some number in her
head, a chain of digits so big it makes my settlement no more than
spit. I get the feeling if she ever reaches zero, she'll leave me, swear
to God: she knows what I'm capable of. We never stay in the
currents that long.

The animals come out at this time of day. A great blue heron
we've come to think of as our own patrols the gravel bar, looking for
any fish Jess might have missed. Chipmunks up in the trees scold
us. A black bear sometimes comes down from the hills, no bigger
than a Russian wolfhound, curious at the smell of trout on the
rocks, too small yet to be of danger. We hoot at it and it crashes
back through the manzanita. Sitting there in the water, I can
almost forget all the bad things; they sink way down to the depths.

When we finally get out, the light is going; I can cup what's left
of it in my hands. The tree shadows stand on long stilts, so many
trees.

"You're the catch," Jess says. "You."

But what I see in this bastard hour, not day, not night, what I
see is her smile and something else in the smirchy orange, swimming under the surface. I can't say. It's only flashes, glints.

I HAVEN'T ALWAYS BEEN faithful. There was a woman once.
Her name—her name isn't important. This was years ago, long
before that blackheart accountant of mine ever dreamt of strip shopping malls. It was thousands of miles from these woods. I wasn't
married to Jess then, the two of us living together, the beginning.

I didn't love the woman, not close. Jess was the one I loved; I only needed one look to know that. When I first saw Jess, I knew exactly what the picture of the rest of my life could be: balanced, watertight.

But the woman, she was messy, desperate, which had its thrill; being with Jess, on the one hand, this needy harpy, the other. Also there was the possibility of getting caught. A brutish feeling like that, a person's truly alive. I wanted to hurt her, hurt everybody. I'm not proud of it.

She'd scream holy hell, too—our loving. One time, the last time, we went at it during her period. It was grainy inside, not the usual sugar, and I came out bloody. She went off for a tampon, some such thing. I looked in the bedside table for a tissue, saw it then in the drawer: a plastic bag big enough to fit over her head and a vial of sleeping pills.

Later she said, "I can't live without you. Really. You can't imagine."

Even then I couldn't help myself. I wanted to afflict her in the worst way. That was what she did to me. I ran from her bed, the house, when she said that to me, about not being able to live without me, left her with her bag and pills. And I told Jess about the nasty business, everything. "You deserve to know," I'd said, but that wasn't it, not really. What I wanted—why I told—was to see the look, the injury, mar her perfect face.

I used to be a red-meat eater back then, I tell you, a real carnivore, liked to put my teeth into people. Now it's only fish.

THERE'S A BIG DAMN fish in these waters—that's what people say. Our neighbor Cockeye Joe for one. A rainbow the size of a small child. *Peyca sulat* is the Indian name for it. Also the long-hair at the store talks about it, except he calls the lunker *big pud*. "It exists. A trout about the size of your old lady," the long-hair says to me. "Truth be told."

We go to Cockeye Joe's stick shack. It's over the hump of hill from our caboose. He tells us stories. I bring whisky. He won't drink from the bottle. I buy a fifth of Early Times at the store, pour it in a jar, tell him I cooked up the mash myself. I don't know if he believes me, probably not; he drinks it, though.

Cockeye Joe isn't his real name. It's *nolti hami-li*. "Eyeing someone with a dark eye," he tells us, what it means. He's solid as a white oak, nearly as tall. *Big*. Old, too. He reminds me of a kite, skin stretched over his bones the way it is.

"All the people are animals," he says, a rumble voice, a kettle of sadness. There are hides on the walls, smell of fire in the shack. It's duskier than twilight—the windows are greased and smoked.

He never looks at Jess when he tells the stories. He's told of how the earth was formed, the theft of daylight, about John Doctor and *wimah*, the grizzly. We want to know about fish, always fish, but Joe only tells what he wants to.

He says, "The people are animals. Never forget." When he talks we see elk and mule deer ranging the land. We live deep in the forest. It's not difficult to picture the days when Wintu walked this earth.

"There was one," he says. "*Peyca sulat*. She was not always this way. A *kul*—this is what she was. Beautiful woman." Joe drinks from the jar, stares off. He tells us the story, how *peyca sulat* was tricked by coyote, the giving of her passion. It's a good story with more twists than the trail up to Lion Lake. "In the end," Joe says, "she cries much from coyote, the trickery. It formed Boulder Creek, her crying. The waters rose and *peyca sulat* turned into the great trout. So much was her sorrow. She swims the creek still."

Joe trails off, drinks the whisky. When that's done, we go.

It's fall outside the shack, the season a shell about to break into a million little pieces, turn colder. Already there are patches of snow up on Billy's Peak. Mornings, chunks of ice wash down the fall line of the river. Soon winter will blow down from Canada, cold and hard.

We've lived in our caboose in the woods for a round of seasons and then some. I'm turning into someone different. Those old hell-born tendencies—I'm throwing them off, like the clothes when we fish.

Jess says nothing on our tramp back through the woods, lost in Joe's story, the *idea* of a fish that big. A woodpecker raps on bark. When I look back at her, there are tears in her eyes, running down her face, over her chin, Jess thinking of the fish-girl. I can see the gold lantern hanging in a window of the caboose now, everything else dark. *We're almost home,* I want to say to her, *almost there. So close.* It's a river coming down her face. I'm afraid she'll swim away.

I HAVE BIG PLANS. The caboose is only the beginning. There's enough money to truck in other trains. We've hardly touched what's left of the settlement. We live on fish.

It's a splendid sight to come through the sugar pines and oaks, through the madrones stooped as hunchbacks, and see the old caboose. It's not red but green as a fir tree, from back east. The rail-road line is written in goldleaf, *Lackawanna,* an Indian name. A ladder climbs to the top, the observation deck. We drink big gin drinks up in the leaves and branches—moonglows, we call the drinks—and we look at the stars.

The rains have come to the woods these days and the fish are biting more than ever. We still stand on the gravel bar naked, fishing, the rain so cold it's almost an electric shock. Boulder Creek runs wild now, more white in the green water, sounds like thunder or bombs going off in a faraway place. The current moves too fast to make ice. We sit after fishing in a deep side pool. Jess looks as if she's still counting down in her head from that big, big number, although sometimes the expression on her face in the polar water tells me that catching fish is enough.

What I want to do is truck up an old sleeper car, a locomotive, too. It'd be brilliant: a string of trains—caboose, sleeper, and locomotive—joined in a neat row, under all these trees. What we'd do is ride the planet, the circuit of seasons. Miraculous. It'd never end. Can you imagine?

I want to tell Jess of the plans, that this is what we have to look forward to. Maybe kids also. You never know. But I don't say anything. I want her to see how much I've changed first, a completely different animal. I'm not sure she does. It's still so new.

We visit Cockeye Joe often, bring jerky and fish we've dried. He's told us how. I'm worried about Joe, the winter months. He's older than dirt; it doesn't seem he can last another season of cold.

He tells us, "Everyone's connected. Our souls. We share them. Dead or alive, it don't matter." This he says to Jess, looks her square, the first time ever. She nods slowly, pins him with her eyes, seems to understand what he's saying, the very heart.

Tonight atop the caboose it's clear after four days of rain. A few clouds pass by, gray as wisps of smoke, night darker than the nap of our black bear, crown of stars up high.

"I'm worried about Joe," I say. "Winter."

Jess is tying a line of terminal tackle, a jig, snap, swivel. She looks at her hands, a factory of motion, says, "What do you think it will take? The test line, I mean. For the fish-girl. *Peyca sulat.*"

My teeth chatter from how cold the moonglow is. The drink is hitting me now. I can feel the caboose riding the earth.

Jess regards me, puts her hand on my arm. Her face relaxes from the hard concentration of working the leader in starlight. "I'm sorry," she says. "What'd you say? Oh, about Joe. Don't worry. All people are animals, right? He knows how to surive, anyway. The last of the Wintu." She goes back to tying.

Right now, up here on this deck, I wonder if I turned the caboose around, if we went back, earth spinning the other way, I wonder if we could get back to the place before the doomed woman. Everything would be different, what I know now.

She says, "I think it's going to take an O'Shaughnessy or maybe a keel-fly hook. Look at me," she says and laughs. And I do — look at her. All I see in the night is angles, tip of her nose, cheekbones, that's all.

I USED TO BE the worst of the cutthroats. Jess doesn't know the half of it. If I wanted something and you were standing before me, gangway. There was no telling how low I'd go. I'd submarine you.

When I first met Jess she didn't want anything to do with me. This was nearly nine years ago. I lied, schemed my way into seeing her; I was the worst of the four-flushers, used to work in advertising. Truth was only a thing that could be bent into a sharp object, a hook to land someone.

In the end, she trusted her initial animal instincts about me. She said, "I don't think this is such a good idea." I went down to my basement after, clamped my ring finger in a vise, wanged a claw hammer down square on the knuckle. The pain was *clarifying*, I tell you, quite possibly the cleanest, most beautiful feeling in my life, so absolute it was. They had to fuse the knuckle; I still can't bend the finger.

Jess visited me in the hospital when she heard about the accident — that was what everybody called it, the accident. Somehow, the finger changed everything, how she saw me, who she thought I was.

I thought being with her would be enough. But the ugly thing inside, you have to kill it—kill it or feed it. It doesn't stop. I fed it the suicide woman, devoured her whole, couldn't help myself.

My accountant also. For years, we'd bilked the government— phony deductions, unreported income, the like. His mistake was skimming off me, the strip shopping mall in Florida. When I discovered, I sued with a mighty vengeance. The thing of it was, he couldn't turn me in for all my dodgy returns. He was my fiduciary; he'd be in deeper yet. It was lovely: go to jail or pay me. I destroyed him.

JESS WANTS THE BIG fish, *peyca sulat*. It's all she can think about these days. Winter is starting to blow into the canyon. We wear loincloths now made of skins, for the cold, the rest of us naked, stippled in gooseflesh. The first dustings of snow cover the granite knobs, the treetops on the property.

She's taken to consulting Cockeye Joe about fishing, wears her loincloth all the time, up to his stick shack even. He doesn't seem to notice, his eyes looking to places that are old and very distant.

"I want to build the willow netting," she says to me, a story that Joe's told earlier. We cut willow brush and weave it, tie it all tightly to a pole. We beat the water with sticks, driving the fish upstream into the roller. The trout, salmon, and suckerfish come from under the banks, out from cracks in rocks. We catch a prodigious amount. The netting quivers, beats, a living thing. Still no *peyca sulat*.

"We're getting close," she says. "This is good." I'm happy to see a fire in her, even if it is about the fish, not me. "We should skin the salmon and grind the bones into flour," she says. "The Wintu way."

When we are not fishing or plotting of fish, we walk the land the way the people did. Jess has her own plans. She wants to build a sweathouse to bleed us of toxins. I want to tell her it's not necessary, all the poison's out of me now.

We don't go to the store these days, haven't seen the long-hair for weeks. We eat what we catch, dry the rest. We still go up to the top of the caboose to watch the stars jitter in the night, but the gin gave out weeks ago.

I can feel the cold down to my bones as we sit in the side pool now. "I think we've been going at this wrong," she says. Water is up to the tip of her chin; I believe she wants to stay submerged forever. "Down there," she says and points to where the creek steps into a wide, still tarn, a flat swelled by rains. "I've seen something way down in the water," she says. "I can feel it. There."

When we get out and stand by the fire I've made, she's all ribs and points, is so beautiful it hurts to look at her. At night I wake in the caboose, the wind a wild thing outside, the washing, washing of the river; rising from my tide of sleep I feel as if we're really moving. I think then that she's changing herself.

The last time we went up to Joe's shack, he was gone. We hiked up days ago, a foot of snow on the ground, more in the high places. The door to the stick shack was wide open. It looked as if nobody had been living there for years, the fire smell gone.

"Where could he be?" I said. "This isn't good."

Jess's eyes glowed, stones in a fire. "All our souls are connected," she said. "It's okay."

WE'RE DOWN AT THE wide tarn when I hook the fish. It's my turn and I cast, let line out. Jess stands at the edge of the pool, a warrior watching the currents. It's nothing more than a gentle tug, what I feel at first. Then the line sings on takeout, goes tight as piano wire.

I dig the rod into my hip, put all two hundred pounds against the diving fish. Jess barks out orders, a drill sergeant. "Let it run," she says. "Tire it out. Don't break the line."

I'm being jerked this way and that.

"It's running toward you," she says. "Don't let it slack."

I reel in fast until I feel tension. The rod is bent into nearly a U.

Jess says, "It's as big as a gal's thigh. All the way around. The biggest fucking fish I've ever seen."

I can't see anything from where I've walked to, way up on the bank. It's sweaty business working the fish, even in my loincloth, in this freezing cold.

The minutes go by and still I see no fish, only the slant of line going into water, rip in the current, that's it. I start to think, There isn't any fish at all. Perhaps it's Cockeye Joe.

Jess gives me a look now so hard, so pointed, it goes to the center of me. "Don't fucking lose that fish," she says. "I mean it."

Seeing this flinty edge, I think maybe she knew all along, about the woman those years ago. Maybe she was only letting me run out line until I jerked on the end of it, snagged. With the bent rod, my numb hands heavy as stone, it makes stupid sense. They looked like each other, Jess and the woman, that was the odd thing, could have been sisters.

Except I hated that woman, always loved Jess, even when I hurt her. The other woman, she flopped around on the sheets, a suckerfish, white belly shining like silver. Made me want to eviscerate her with myself.

It happened later, the suicide, long after I told Jess—and not with pills or her plastic bag. She filled her tub with water, balanced a trunk full of rocks on the square lip of it, climbed into the tub, reached up and pulled the trunk, rocks and all, on top of her. It wasn't because of me but someone else; that was what we heard. But who can actually know?

I think of her as I wrestle this great fish now, *peyca sulat.* I can see the blue above the blue she must have seen under there, air above the lip of mirrored water, how it must have turned gray, then black. And then it was only a tub filled with rocks and sorrow.

Jess is telling me to walk further up the bank now, to walk the fish out of the water. But there is too much weight down there. I can't lift all of it. My arms have gone rubbery from the effort, a stinging in my hands. Just when it seems too much for me to bear, the line snaps. I fall back into snow.

When I stand again Jess is there. I want to tell her that there will be another day to hoist up that fish. We'll have another chance. But I don't say anything. Her face is still as a pool. I can see all the way to the bottom. What she's thinking about on the way back to our beached train in these woods, what she's thinking about is all the things we've lost, the things that were, everything that could have been.

The Ames Coil

I MISSED THE WET falls most. That Trinity rain could come
down, come down like the sky'd cracked open, whole sluiceway
spilling through, a million arrows of rain falling straight as a dead
man. That kind of wet.

If I told him, Ames wouldn't have heard me even without
them metal detector earmuffs on. He'd been a desert creature since
the navy, forever. It was all he knew.

He was sweeping out along the basin now, pappy beard falling
down below his chin, like deer moss, uneven cutoffs, hair on his
legs thick as troops of army ants.

The desert scrabble rolled all the way to the Shoshones, the
sky.

We were looking for buried treasure, leastways Ames. "Might
just find us the fleshpots of Egypt," he'd say. "If you know where to
look, that is."

And it was a true thing that he'd unearthed some unusual
booty. Mostly it was washing machine drums, rusted-out basketball
hoops, tears of culvert, rebar, sometimes pocket change, barbed

wire, busted wheel rims, metal that didn't look like it came from anything on the planet. "Must be from a spaceship," he'd say about that. Me, I'd wonder what a washing machine was doing so deep in the basin.

He scared up a sage grouse waving his device now, didn't even notice the ruckus, the yellow dirt suspended long after. He just kept fanning away from the county road, the Big Hot, eyes on the talc like he was reading it.

Sometimes he stopped, when the needle on the gauge juked, and he'd paw at the ground. Then Frank and Bing would swoop down from the Scout at roadside. The dogs were sitting with me amongst the red rocks in the shade, looking at me in a floral sundress that had seen better days, grinning like wolves, killers. When Ames started kicking at the dirt, they'd scramble off, the two black-and-whites shooting across the basin, shoulder to shoulder. All three of them would create a shower of dirt.

The dog that'd free the scrap from the ground, he'd parade with it in his mouth, shake it like it was some vole he'd caught, a living thing. They'd tire of the game after that, come wagging back to me at the car where I was reading a mother dime novel, sitting under a bonnet to keep the sun off, as if that'd make any difference.

Ames had more patience than those dogs and me combined, was always sure fortune was under the next greasewood bush. It was just a matter of finding it. "We're going to dig up all of Nevada," he said. "If'n that's what it takes."

He'd rigged an awning that folded out neat as could be from the roofline of the Scout to afford me some shade. I went along first because it was Ames, second because it was a settling thing out there, so much sky, so different from Trinity, where everything was choked with bark and rock; and water, everywhere water.

Mostly it was side trips. Sometimes we camped under the sky, a modest pinyon fire for cooking; so many stars going, they looked plugged in. It seemed then maybe there *was* something valuable in that ground.

If there was, Ames never found it, but not to hear him tell it. He was absolutely delighted with the flotsam we'd tote back. "Part of my plan," he'd say and snap the corner of his mouth, like he had something tasty inside. "All part of the plan."

He lived on the money the VA mailed him, something to do with his skin, I thought. His face was pocked as a sponge. He never talked about it. To hold up my end, I cleaned and cooked.

Anyway, that money was just holding him until the plans took shape. Just what that was, he wasn't saying. I'd see him back in the Airstream, the little hours of night, drawing up his ideas on paper the size of bedsheets. Sometimes from my room in the shack across the plot of Mexican tea shrub, I'd see him on the balcony he jerry-built, Ames looking at a salmon dawn, morning planet still blinking way up high.

He was no more than a speck out on the high plateau now, him and the metal detector. I could see that smile of his even if I couldn't see his face, baseball cap on backward, faded tattoo on his upper arm—*Hannah or Hell*, it looked to read, but it could have been something else entirely. He waved to us and Bing lifted his head, debating whether he wanted to leave the shade or no. Ames gave the thumbs-up, dug his heel into the dirt, and the two dogs were off, flat-out, reaching across desert, joining him in the excavation.

There were worse ways to spend a day and I'd done some of them. After I ran off from Trinity, I picked berries in the Central Valley with migrants. When the season was done, I blew east, over Fallon way, and worked as a sensuous masseuse, squeezing fat middle-aged men's wieners. Next I worked past Carson in a road-house titty bar until the owner told me what was supposed to shake on me didn't, what wasn't did. "It's what happens," he'd said. "Women your age."

After that I'd had enough crap jobs and drove as far as the tank of my ruinous car would take me. That was Thirteenmile, the parking lot of a roadhouse by the same name.

"Hattie? That's an old name," Ames had said to me inside the bar, which was how I felt, a thousand years.

"Just a girl from Hungry Horse," I'd said, waiting to order. "Trinity, California." I could have said more. About Gordon Lee, about Chance. I didn't.

We played a dice game he called Mex on the burl bartop, slapping down bug juice the whole night. "Forty-four," he'd say, looking at my pair of dice. "Reggie Jackson. You drink." Or "Looky, it's Elvis in the army, fifty-six. I guess it's me who's thirsty this time."

It went on this way until we closed the place. When we come out, it was past two in the morning and the desert sky was spinning a little from all the drink. "I got a bunk," he'd said. "Nothing much. It's inside from the cold, though."

We climbed into the front of his piebald Rambler. I figured I knew what was coming, had done worse, though probably none uglier than this one, ratty hair, chewed-up face as long as the month of July.

He didn't say much. The night swallowed up everything, the broken mesa heading out to meet it in every direction. After a handful of miles he turned off onto a dirt road and after some twists I saw a lone bumper car setting right in the middle of the sage. Then we topped a rise and it came into sight: a triplet of Airstreams, the silver glinting somewhat from the moon, each one attached to the other, like docking spaceships.

That was the last I remembered, me pretty soggy from all the bug juice. I thought it was a dream when I woke the next morning, the Airstreams. I came to in a little pine shack, on top of an army cot, clothes still on, no Ames anywhere.

But when I went outside there was them three cigar-shaped trailers, just as I remembered. There was plenty more to fill the eyes, too. I saw a great big whirligig with two dogs hooked up to it, the dogs off to a fine trot, the contraption wheezing out "Camptown Races" as it spun, dogs making happy circles.

Behind that was wooden struts of a tower, huge tank perched on top. Off to the other side of the Airstreams was a yard of metal covering the ground like grass, layer of silver and rust. Ames was in the middle of it, combing through with a rake. There were other things, too, steel poles from bathtubs with watering cans welded to the ends, things I can't even describe to this day.

I couldn't take it all in, what with the previous night's tequila. Later he showed me a needle instrument he'd built that makes a spookish noise if you spin your hands in front of it. And a satellite dish that was half-made and left, inspired by some inventor.

Ames gave me a little high sign wave, a flip of the hand, from the middle of that acre of metal when he first seen me that morning after, little flip of his hand. It was the same wave he gave me now as he and Frank and Bing came back toward the Scout across scrub, dragging what looked to be a bale of cyclone fencing. It took minutes for them to pick their way across the rabbit brush.

I could see Ames beaming like he'd won the sweepstakes. "A find," he said when he finally made it roadside and put the fencing with the rest of the scraps. The dogs were wiggling with his excitement.

"Who'd a thought," I said. "Who'd a thought anybody would call that mess treasure?"

"Nikola Tesla," he said. "That's who."

Then we didn't say anything, just looked over the stretch of basin. Late afternoon was coming on, sun dampened, sky grown heavy with desert clouds. The air was sharp and chilled and sparklesome.

We watched the rain gathering over the Shoshones, that water never reaching us on the ground. It meant to. It was coming down overhead, streaky and gray, striping the air like comb marks. But that thirsty middle air must have sopped it up, something. It was a mystery to me where it went, the rain, how the Nevada dirt under us could stay dry as a fact.

At that moment, I thought for all of Ames's secret plans and inventions, I would have been happy just if he could make it rain. It was ten months in the desert and I'd hardly seen it ever. It must have, though. The hefty catchment that sat up on the tower behind the Airstreams had to be gathering something.

I said now, "A person could go out of business selling umbrellas. A place like this." The basin was filled with lakes of shadows but no water.

"Oh, I don't know," Ames said. "Plenty of uses for a good umbrella."

I'D HAD MY SHARE of men both before and after Chance Brophy. Not a one of them was like Ames DeWalt, not close. We lived like brother and sister out on that gila spread of his. It was a comfortable thing, too, after a lifetime of looking into mirrors, dressing yourself up for men.

Ames and me fell into an easy rhythm. I lived out in the pine shed, bought the groceries, set out meals, kept the generator full and running spry, once he showed me how. It seemed as good a place as any to be, until I could puzzle out what was next.

Ames, he was working in earnest on the plans that were going to be his salvation. I'd been seeing that lone bumper car on the landscape for going on three months now and still he hadn't told me what was up. Part of him wanted to—I could see that, the itchy, knotted expression his face sometimes took.

Come February, he planned a trip to a junkyard out Cold Springs way, up 50, the loneliest road in America. You hear it from Ames, it was like we were making a religious journey. "An amazing sight, the yard," he said. "Switches, step-ups, modulators. Just the tip of the iceberg."

I said, "Sounds like you can find anything there."

"Anything," he said.

"Well, I might just have to go," I said. "Might find something I didn't even know I was looking for."

He laughed. "You'll see, Hattie. You'll see. Got a café right outside the yard, too. Defy you to find a better split-pea soup in the state of Nevada. It's got a flavoring I can't quite identify. Bacon, maybe. Can't say."

The day came, February 16. It was one of them blue desert mornings, air cold, the kind you think you can see forever. We left the dogs back on the property.

There's nothing like driving the desert. Ames'd tuned up the Scout the day before. It rode smooth as a gyro on 50, the two of us clipping along, yellow basin coming at us like the bottom of a cereal bowl.

The weeks of junkyard conversation had me in a keen mood as well. We didn't talk during the drive, mostly kept to our own thoughts, an edge of awkwardness in the car. That was how it was whenever we left the trio of Airstreams for town, the shortest breath of unease between us.

I had a warm lonesome feeling on the drive, the good kind.

Right then with the junipers outside the window fuzzy as pilled wool, life didn't seem so big or like it was the saddest thing in the world, only that it was your own.

I thought of my little Gordon Lee, a boy who'd never be any more than three years old, never, Gordon in that home in Trinity, dirty hair falling over his eyes in ropy spikes, crying a creek in flood stage that last time. I wanted to tell Ames about Gordon Lee then, about what it was like to have a little boy who'd never say much more than "Mommy." But how do you tell someone that you'd run out on a kid like that? There just aren't words.

The junkyard was indeed a vision, the size of ten football fields. There was a mountain of car batteries tall as a house and all manner of metal and steel. I could see what Ames was modeling his own yard after.

He went off. I toured the rows, stepping over brown oxide puddles. The crusher was like a demented kiddie ride, how it squashed everything down to a neat square. I watched two truckers up in a cab circle their rig, back up, drop their load of flattened autos.

They pulled forward and stepped down to watch also. The trucker said to me, "You remind me of somebody." He winked at his friend.

"You don't remind me of anybody," I said. I started to look for Ames. A worker up in the cab of the crusher fired it up, gunned the motor; the monster began eating the load.

"You sure?" he said over the clatter. "Dead ringer for someone in Fallon." The friend got a smile. The metal was screaming in the crusher, burnt wire smell, too.

I knew what they meant, the parlor. A job like massage, faces were one thing you didn't remember.

"You remind me of someone in Fallon," he said again.

"You remind me of a headache," I said. The friend with the stupid smile laughed. I left them to look for Ames. He was in the corner of the yard with a full cart of equipment. We loaded the mess into the Scout, then drove to the café.

It was true what he said: I couldn't say I'd had a better split-pea soup. Ames was crowing about his pile of equipment, the price he'd gotten it for. In spite of himself, he began telling me about the plans.

"It's a high-frequency transformer," he said, his burry voice. He told me about that Tesla fellow again, how he hatched the idea for some kind of coil in the clear, dry Colorado Springs air.

"Colorado?" I said.

"That's right," he said. "Not too big a leap of the imagination from right here. One thing we have, it's clear, dry air."

He was wound up. "It's like a soup," he said, stirring his bowl, "what I'm thinking of. A polyphase motor of a sort that hasn't been seen."

I was nodding at Ames, a woodpecker, understanding only a fraction of it, something to do with electric pulses, radiowaves, magnetism. His back was to the door, so he didn't see the two sour truck jockeys come in when they did. They sat up at the counter, that pair, off to the side of Ames.

I thought the clowns were going to come by the table, tell Ames what it was I used to do before I drove the road to Thirteenmile. I was smiling at him all the while, him talking science, but inside I was playing out the possibilities of such a scene, thinking my snug life at his spread was about to fly.

Those boys stayed at the counter, though. Ames never saw them. One of them unfolded a napkin, held it to his chin, imitating Ames's scraggy beard.

I was sorry for Ames then. He was going on about arc lighting and alternating current and what I saw across the table wasn't an electronic visionary but a little boy telling me his plans of winging to the moon. Seeing those slugs having their fun, I wanted to scoop him up, tell him he could do anything, anything he wanted.

The truckers didn't let up, flapping their mouths like Ames talking. I wanted to get us out of there before he saw. "It's a long ride," I said. "Soup's on me. My treat." I said, "You're right. It was bacon."

He went to the Scout and I up to the counter. I turned to the boys after paying, said, "He's a veteran. Probably a hero, no doubt."

The one with the stupid smile looked up at me. "I can show you something heroic," he said. "You probably remember."

I said, "I don't think between the two of you boys, you can muster up a serious hard-on. That's what I think."

When I got out to the car, Ames was looking at the boys waving at me through the window. He said, "Those two giving you trouble?"

I said, "Not anymore."

We drove 50, the day hotter, smell of machined parts in the car. The sky was an ocean that held no water, that deep and blue. For the first time, I was embarrassed about the work I did back in Fallon. Also I was surprised at the tilt my feelings had taken in the café, me not wanting the truckers, or anybody, to squeeze Ames through a tube.

"I liked the Tesla stuff," I said. "The way you talk."

He gave a flat smile.

Just past four-thirty, we crested a bluff below Hickison Summit. Ames pulled onto the shoulder. The land spilled out below, the yellow dirt and sage and juniper scrub rolling to every point of the compass, early night clouds out now, dropping shadows on the mesas, like inky pools, the shadows.

The first planets were winking on. At that time of day, it was easy to mistake those lights for UFOs. "I think we're in for it," I said. "Little green men."

Ames nodded. "They laughed at him, Tesla," he said. "He was pulling in radiowaves from space. Said it was intelligent life from Venus and Mars. Turned out he was right, the radiowaves. Even if it wasn't Martians and Venutians."

I wanted to say something smart, to let him know I knew his plans were dead-on.

Ames looked out the windshield. "Course," he said, "it didn't help matters much that Tesla had this aversion to billiard balls."

I smiled, said, "I know you're right. What you said before." I wanted to pat him, let him know I believed. My hands stayed fixed in my lap. In the dark, his face was ridged as the mesa.

"The truth," he said. "Scared of cue balls and pearl earrings."

"No doubt," I said.

"Truth is one thing you don't flirt with," he said. "You get yourself married to it right away."

We watched a section of moon get visible, hang in the sky, a funny buck tooth. And I didn't know what to think, whether this plan of Ames's was gospel or cue balls and earrings or what.

BACK IN TRINITY, I used to be married to a man so handsome, he'd hurt your eyes, the most skilled logger in all the woods. Technically speaking, I was still married to him.

We had a life together, a piece of heaven in that green world, had a cottage right on the river, used to have to cross a rope-and-plank bridge to get to it.

Chance had built the whole place himself. The first year, before the cottage went up, we lived in a pygmy trailer on the side of the road. He'd get the boys to drop off extra loads from jobs, had a little mill for the pines we took down from our own property. It was a special feeling to walk around, say, "This deck here, it came from the stand up on the rise. The Doug fir for the board-and-batten was left over from Long Canyon." And so on.

I used to sit on the deck over the oxbow and the river would talk to me. In spring, after the rains and melt, it washed down brown as coffee, rolling boulders, sounding like a bowling alley when it got big. Into summer and fall, the level dropped and the water was green and fast, carried a cold, wet wind.

It came to me up on the deck that this was what I always thought marriage would be, back when I was twelve or so, living with someone like Chance, a man so big, you could lose yourself inside his hug, and it was okay to be lost like that.

I used to say to him, "You're my last Chance." I'd say, "After you, I'm out of Chances." We'd laugh, the thought that there could be something after this.

Those days he was a good man. There was some fooling with drugs but it wasn't a problem then. Most of them boys on the helicopter crew were using. Come late fall, they did everything they could to squeeze in as much work as possible, trying to beat closeout. "Be flying until the first snow flies," they'd say and get all geeked up. When the season was finished, it took some weeks for Chance to wear off that crank edge. He always did. Then we'd have the winter for ourselves.

He was the best of that lot, could spot a stand of old growth from five thousand feet, easy as coal in a snowdrift, amazing. He had the knack.

Sometimes in summer, months before the scrambling days near closeout, I'd hear his copter way up there and get nectary inside. It was all I could do to wait for him to get back, and when he did, we'd go down to the water, him still full of sap, sawdust in the hair of his arms, like snowflakes. When he came inside me under the trees it was electricity. Then Chance'd go in the icy current, his long body stepping into the folds of water.

There wasn't any one reason why things died. Gordon Lee was part of it, to be sure, little boy like that, makes you wonder where he came from. Even so, he was a beautiful one, filled with troubles.

He was petrified of rain hammering on our tin roof. He could run all day, usually toward trouble, got himself injured in more ways than one can imagine, never learned how to control his body. When he got too big for diapers, I had to sew my own.

Chance acquired a flat look after Gordon Lee was born, seemed to stare beyond Trinity, him thinking, no doubt, it was the drugs that brought the problems on. But he loved the boy also, would go to him the moment he got home from the trees, take him out on the deck, tell him what went down that day.

Chance developed all these ideas about how to make it work. "I'm going to build us another cottage here," he said one night in bed. "Get a nurse for the boy. Full-time. We'll be a regular family. Just wait."

He worked like a pack mule for extra money after that, took any job available during the winter, began messing more with crank to keep the hours going. It was difficult, seeing him whipping himself for something he might not have done. And he lost his sureness. Before the drugs got bad, he could walk among the trees and still look tall, but no more.

Come closeout in Gordon Lee's fifth year, he kept flying, got the bright idea of starting his own lab. "It's a shitpot of money," he said. "I'm telling you, Hattie. A shitpot. No more slaving jobs." He had it all figured out, would set up in the abandoned Milkmaid mine. He was wire-thin by then from all the crank.

I said, "Chance, this isn't the way. There are homes for kids like him." I was tired of sleeping next to a man whose engine never shut down, sparks flying off him always.

"There's only one home for Gordon Lee," he said. After that he trucked the equipment up to Milkmaid, stayed the season, cooking up crank.

By March I hadn't seen my husband in over a month. The rains came, a bad year, water climbing to right under the rope-and-plank bridge. I believed we were going to wash away.

I piled Gordon Lee into the car, drove up to the mine, hoped I could shame Chance. He must have heard the sound of the engine deep in the drift. I saw him peeking out the opening, gun cocked, a shocking thing, how he looked, ancient, bent. He was vibrating from how much he was using, kept the gun pointed on us even after he saw who it was.

"This isn't about Gordon Lee anymore," I said.

Rain was washing over his head, his great big chest only hollow then, pants soiled worse than the boy's ever got.

He pointed the muzzle at the ground, said, "I'm your last Chance. Go on, say it, Hattie."

I said, "It doesn't have to be this way."

"If I could," he said and stopped. I thought he was going to talk about turning right, back to how it was.

He said, "If I could cook up a recipe that good . . ." He pointed to Gordon Lee. "If I could cook that up, we could retire." Then he went back down the hole.

I put Gordon Lee in a home the next day. And I fled, rains coming down, trees snapping in a northerly the whole way out. And I told myself I didn't ever want to see rain again, not ever.

IT WAS LATE AFTERNOON, end of February. The long desert

shadows were out, near eggplant sky. Ames's yard of metal glowed in the last light. "One thing about Nikola Tesla," he said, two of us at his picnic table. "Went off his nut at the end. Said he could make a death ray. Said it'd zap a million soldiers in an instant."

It was like Nikola himself was living on the property with us then. Ames could go off for a good twenty minutes, easy. When it wasn't that, it was the Ames coil, what he called his secret contrivance.

He'd told me more about it after the trip to the junkyard. "It's a resonant air-core transformer," Ames had said. The best I could make out, it was some sort of tower that gave off a number of electric frequencies, the idea being that the very air we breathed would conduct power.

"Won't need plugs, batteries, that generator, nothing," he'd said. "It'd be a new age to be sure. Could run electric cars off it. Just think."

And I did. And it sounded coot crazy, the notion that a desert rat, surviving in the basin with the lizards and greasewood, drawing what living he could off the VA, the notion that someone like that could change how the world spun.

I didn't let on. I helped him pour the footings for the towers, dug trenches below the water tank. The coil was to go up in front of the catchment. We put the dogs' paws into the cement before the rock set, signed our names, too. "You're in on the foundation, Hattie," he'd said. "The ground floor."

Now at the picnic table, I listened to him go on about Tesla, February sky magic, a dark bruise that faded over the Shoshones.

Ames was all eyes and hair. "Look at me," he said, "the way my mouth runs."

"It's not so bad," I said.

"Even so," he said. He reached down to pet Bing and Frank.

"You're quiet, Hattie." He lit the lantern on the table. It spit, globe pulsing until the mantle warmed.

I said, "I'm turning forty. March eleventh."

He became a pumpkin smiling, yellow light, mouthful of nub teeth, cracked lips pulled back. "How about that," he said. "I been a lot worse things than forty years."

Frank and Bing wrestled with each other, white ruffs, blazes, teeth. I said, "Forty. Doesn't seem to add up." I thought about Chance. During my first Nevada days, I expected to see him boiling across the high country, yellow tail of dirt behind his El Camino. The picture I'd had in my mind, he'd be sturdy again from pounding wedges, hoisting chainsaws. Gordon Lee was there also, cured. The little one would have surprised me, how he'd grown. He'd have had a baseball cap on, would have talked a streak, telling me everything in his six-year-old head.

Ames said now, "What do you want, your birthday?"

I said, "Too old for that."

"I hope not," he said.

A half moon peaked over his shoulder. The dogs quieted, crawled under the table. The generator hummed behind the Airstreams and clothes I'd hung on the line earlier snapped in a breeze that blew down shivery and dry from the range.

"How about this," he said. "You go to town, get a pedicure, facial, what have you. On me."

"Oh, I don't know," I said.

The wind breathed hop sage, shook the chimes Ames had tacked up over one of his windows. I wondered what foolishness Nikola Tesla was saying to him right then.

And I kept wondering into early March, days growing long-limbed, light creeping into evening. I thought Ames was going to break, he was working so on his coil, stopping just for sleep and meals and only occasionally. Sometimes when I looked at him, I didn't see Ames but a shadow of Chance's face, that last time at Milkmaid.

I DROVE THE RAMBLER to Ames's mailbox out on the county road the day before my birthday. His benefit check came the tenth of every month. "Keep the Indians at bay," I called to him from outside. "I'm going for reinforcements." He gave me his high sign through the window. Frank and Bing were beside themselves with glee, thinking I was taking them on another scrap-hunting expedition. It'd been so long since we'd gone.

Inside the car, Bing made nose prints looking out the window. Frank watched me. "What," I said to him. "You think I'm stealing this heap?"

The dog raised an ear.

"Fine watchdog you are," I said.

The Rambler rocked over chuckholes and washboards. A black-tailed hare bobbed out from a brush heap. Both dogs perked.

"I don't know how you do it, Frank," I said. "Bing's the stupid one. But you. Living out here in this country." The dog edged toward me. "I get it," I said. "You think that time doesn't go by out here, that you're living the same day over and over." I rubbed the velvet of his ear. "Pretty good philosophy," I said. "For a dog."

The VA envelope was there as expected; I recognized the blue type. There was something else in the box, too, which I assumed was for Ames until I looked. My name was printed across the front. During my entire stay at his place I'd gotten but one letter, a Nevada driver's license.

I figured it was a birthday card from Ames. Then I saw the printing, crabbed and falling down to the right. And I knew. Chance.

I let Frank and Bing out of the car. They ran to a stand of creosote and mule fat, looking to chase hares. I leaned against the fender and listened to the engine tick slower and slower. I didn't open the envelope, just held it out in front of me, the brown, droughty land framing it on all sides.

The return address was *California Correctional Facilities*. "You've gone from one hole to another," I said to the envelope but still couldn't open it. I thought on all the things Chance could possibly say. I decided it wasn't anything I hadn't told myself already.

There was only a picture inside. Gordon Lee. I didn't recognize him at first. His hair had turned brown. He had thick black glasses on, was looking at something off to the side of the camera. Portland Trailblazer cap on his head.

And I was wrong: this was worse than anything I ever called myself. And I tried to cry but nothing came.

When I got back, I slid the VA envelope under the Airstream's door, went down to the pine shed. I tried to sleep, didn't think I could, but must have because I woke to knocking.

I opened the door to Ames. The day was going fast behind him. "It's your birthday eve," he said.

I said, "Okay, so what's the good news?"

He laughed. "You're a one, Hattie. Me and the boys got a little surprise for you."

I followed him out to the Airstreams and saw. He'd strung colored lights everywhere, up the legs of the water tower, around the top of the dogs' whirligig, the length of the three trailers. It looked like the county fair with the sky going dusky like that.

"You got work to do," I said.

He said, "Not tonight." There was shy embarrassment on his

face. "I made that appointment for you also," he said. "The salon in town. Tomorrow."

Ames wouldn't hear of any thank yous. He got a pinyon and cottonwood fire going in the oil drum. When the coals were shining red, he put a lamb over the fire, potatoes wrapped in aluminum foil amongst the embers, skewers of vegetables, too.

"Don't you even think of clearing this," he said when we were done. "Just stay."

He came back with a bottle of bug juice and we threw dice, played Mex just like the first time, game after game, until I got sloppy and my dice went off the table.

"You hold your liquor better than you hold your dice," he said. He went and hooked the dogs up to the lighted go-round and "Camptown Races" sawed away, Frank and Bing stepping lively. The wind came blowing down the dish of basin. It reminded me of the river back in Trinity, the washing sound.

When Ames returned to the table, I said, "I got a boy. I never told you." And then I did. He gave me a level look the whole time I described Gordon Lee's problems, the kind of home he was in, what it was like with a child like that. I didn't tell him about Chance or the drugs or the photo that came in the mail today, only Gordon Lee.

When I was done, Ames said, "That reminds me of something." I was sure he was going to tell another Nikola Tesla story. He said, "I used to have this parakeet. Would clip its wings. Every month or so they'd grow out and I'd take the bird outside, give it a taste of flying. I'd call it and it'd land right on my finger." Ames showed me.

"This one day," he said, "Crackers is flying and I see this hawk high up in the sky. I call Crackers to me. 'Crackers,' I'm saying. 'Get down from that water tower. Damn hawk up there.'"

The melody to "Camptown Races" was going slower now. Ames looked over to Bing and Frank. "Anyway," he said. "Bird's having a fine old time, making like he doesn't hear me. Meantime that hawk's gliding lower. Shit-for-brains parakeet doesn't have a clue. It was over faster than you'd expect. Hawk snatched him right off that tower."

Ames squinted one eye at me. "Here's the thing," he said. "Hawk'll fly off with its prey, won't kill until several miles out. Well, that hawk's heading away and I hear Crackers. He's saying, 'Ames.' That's the only talk he knew. I'm hearing, 'Ames, Ames, Ames.' And it's getting fainter and fainter. Then nothing."

The fire cracked in the drum. We listened to night for a while, coyotes deep in the basin yipping to one another. Ames went to unhitch the dogs. He came back with a cassette player and played some old-time music with trumpets that talked at you.

He said, "The pleasure of this dance?" We shuffled around, neither of us knowing any proper steps, dogs trailing us. He smelled of pinyon and sage.

"It's not going too good," he said in my ear. "The Ames coil."

"It will," I said. "I know it."

Even with his head so close, I could hardly hear him. "No," he said. It was the saddest thing in the world how it came out, muffled and wet.

I rubbed his back to gentle him. We turned slow together. I thought about that poor little parakeet. I don't know why. I just had this bird's-eye picture of Ames way down on the ground, standing there helpless, watching the hawk fly off.

I hummed in his ear, moved my hands along his back. Ames made a sound in his throat. I kissed his neck.

He said, "No."

"It's okay," I said, "okay." I moved my hands on his back again.

He went to pull off. "Shhh," I said and held him. "It's okay."

Then I touched him, below. And there was nothing there, nothing, only pants fabric that bunched in my hands. And I stood for a moment, stockstill, my hand remaining there, holding only denim.

He fell away from me to the ground then, curled up, cried and cried. Frank and Bing went to lick his face, his sobbing going bubbly, the dogs in a knot around him.

I watched the spectacle but couldn't think of anything to do or say. And I followed his festive lights back to the pine outbuilding, fell asleep thinking maybe I hadn't put my hands in the *right* place, maybe that was it. Or maybe it was all the drink we'd had.

THE NEXT MORNING THERE was a cotton sky over the mesa. When I slinked out to the Rambler to go to town for my salon appointment, I didn't see any activity in the Airstream, no Frank or Bing, either, only a picnic table full of bottles from last night, strings of lights that were extinguished.

I can't say I remembered much from the twenty-mile drive. The scene from last night kept running on a loop in my head, Ames broken on the ground, just his dogs for comfort. Remembering made me shudder yet.

The ladies in the salon hadn't ever seen anyone so in need of their services. "I guess I've been left out in the sun too long," I said to them. I got the treatment, my hair washed then given a rinse and a cutting, a facial and a coat of avocado cream that hardened up like mud, my cracked nails buffed and done, even my feet.

"You're a new woman," the beautician said to me before I left. When I got back to the Rambler, I looked at myself in the rearview mirror. "Still you," I said. "Just all dressed up with no place to go."

And that got me thinking. I was driving back, windshield full of brown and scrub, and I believed I could see clear past the desert to somewhere green, wet. I kept thinking and the idea got easier to hold on to. Running would be so easy. The old familiar feeling rose up in my blood. I could drive the Rambler all the way to Ely, ditch the car, send Ames word about where it was, then just fly.

It was good, the plan. By the time I was winding down 50, it was a done deal. I was already hatching ideas on what was next. Then I saw it, way off in the basin, Ames's Scout, like a mirage.

I was telling myself to keep going, keep going. But I stopped and sat at the wheel roadside and looked at it all the way across the yellow dirt. Then I got out and started walking toward it.

It took half an hour, how far they were from the road. With the sun beating down, me stepping over sage and creosote, up and down washes, I could feel all the salon work beginning to wilt.

And then there was Ames. He was carrying an umbrella overhead for shade, little dangly wind chimes hanging off the spokes, pile of Coke bottles nearby, the green going to blue from the sun, Frank and Bing romping.

We didn't say anything for the longest time, only watched each other. He said finally, "If you looked any nicer, you'd give me the vapors, Hattie." He had an expression of wonder on his face that was pure genius, a look I'd remember for a year and a half.

By then we'd built a little extension onto the pine shed, a deck for me to sit on when I read my romance novels. One afternoon I glanced up from the page and saw in fact it wasn't the same every day in the mesas. You had to look close, but it did change, white around the edges in winter, green tint in early spring that went to gold and then brown.

The Ames coil was erected by then, too, one freezer rack and junked car hood at a time. It was right in front of the water tower as planned. Finally the day came when it was time to turn it on and make history.

Ames waited for evening, a royal desert sunset, first planets coming out. "Just in case the Martians and Venutians are watching," he said. He threw the big switch and that thing started whirring and bucking. The dogs barked at the coil that now was snapping green and blueish sparks, kicking up a racket.

All of a sudden a big ball of light lifted off the coil, vibrated in the air for a second, then jumped the gap up to the galvanized tank on the tower. I felt the explosion down to my teeth. And the water came down and down through the split the spark made, a flood in the desert, water pouring over the coil for minutes. Then there was just smoke and no more noise.

Ames was hushed. He had that same look of wonder on his face, too. Real quiet, he said, "Did you see that? It was a miracle."

And it was, that something so wondrous could grow out of the desert floor, the Ames coil. For one slim moment, its electricity had filled the night.